Dear Great American Writers School

Dear Great American Writers School

Sherry Bunin

Houghton Mifflin Company • Boston 1995

Copyright © 1995 by Sherry Bunin

Library of Congress Cataloging-in-Publication Data

Bunin, Sherry.
Dear Great American Writers School/by Sherry Bunin.
p. cm.
Summary: Fourteen-year-old Bobby Lee's letters to a correspondence
school describe her life in a small Kentucky town during World War
II and her growth as a person and as a writer.
ISBN 0-395-71645-4
[1. Authors—Fiction. 2. Letters—Fiction. 3. World War,
1939–1945—United States—Fiction. 4. Kentucky—Fiction.]
I. Title
PZ7.B915155De 1995 94-27265
[Fic]—dc20 CIP
AC

The lines on page 88 are from
"Ashes of Life" by Edna St. Vincent Millay.
From COLLECTED POEMS, HarperCollins.
Copyright 1917, 1945 by Edna St. Vincent Millay.

Printed in the United States of America
10 9 8 7 6 5 4 3 2 1

In memory of Helen Scott-Harman

Liberty magazine
January 1944

Twin Branch, Ky.

January 3, 1944

Dear Great American Writers School,

Today I read your advertisement in *Liberty* magazine and hope you people can help me with my life. I write stories all the time. I can write 5, sometimes 6, in a day. "Murder and Mayhem" stories used to be my best. They called them that on the cover of the true detective magazines where I sent a story once about a bloody ax murder that took place right here in Twin Branch. The murderer was never brought to justice, but everyone knows it was Bill Farley who murdered his wife, Hilda, and not some hobo off a C&O caboose the way Bill Farley tells it.

Bill Farley's been county sheriff as long as anyone can remember. He's quick-tempered and mean as a pistol if you dare spit on the sidewalk. I changed all the names in my story and put the location in Nome, Alaska, the farthest place I could think of at the time, because I know better than mess with a man who'd ax his wife for burning the biscuits.

It turned out it didn't matter because none of those magazines said they wanted to publish it. I've quit writing detective stories and now I write just plain stories like you read in *Liberty* magazine. I carry those little spiral notebooks, no bigger than a person's hand, and when I see something cute or hear a spicy remark, I write it down and keep track of it for stories that come to me sometimes in the middle of the night.

Thelma Thompson is a person who says a lot of spicy things I keep track of. Thelma quit the high school, where I still go, making a big mistake in her life. All she does now is hang around the First National Bank with a bunch of ancient men, smoking cigs and choking the neck of a Coke bottle. It's a puzzlement how she can stand to listen to them old guys complain about working long hours at the Triple H and brag on how much beer they drank the night before at the Bluegrass Cafe. You'd never hear them talk about the war and what President Roosevelt's up to. You won't catch them reading a newspaper. I bet if you was to ask that bunch, "What do you think about that guy Hitler?" they'd say, "Don't know a Hitler. He must work the night shift!"

Thelma does have her reasons for being friendly with that bunch. I've heard her say, "Anybody got change for a Coke?" or "I need a pack of Luckies," and, I'll tell you, those old guys dig into their pockets like she's their wife on payday.

Thelma is good for stories, all right. On Saturdays, she dresses up in a white skirt with black dots big as old cat eyes, and the skirt so tight, you'd think she'd been born in it. Then she wobbles in a pair of spiky-heel shoes and parades up and down Franklin Street. Saturday is when everybody and their cousin comes to shop in Twin Branch. As soon as the hillbilly boys spot Thelma, they whistle and stomp their feet like wild things. They holler, "Hi, good looking" and "Wanna shack up, sweet pea?"—rude things like that, which don't impress Thelma none. She sticks up her nose like she's smelling clouds, paying them no mind. I have to admire the way Thelma snubs those hillbillies. I got no use for them myself.

Thelma doesn't act that way with me. She sees me and screeches like she's a hillbilly herself. "Scram, you snoopy string bean!" she'll say. "Don't come snooping around me!"

"Aw, Thelma, don't be like that," I say, as nice as a preacher. "I like listening to you. You're an interesting person to listen to."

"You write it all down, don't you?" she says, her eyes flashing fierce little green lights that don't scare me.

"Sure," I confess, "but you got to consider I'm a writer. Writing down what people say is my job."

"Your job is working in your daddy's store selling jockstraps," she snaps right back, putting her hands on her skinny hips like Bette Davis acting evil in the movies. "And I wouldn't brag about working in that diddly old store if I was you."

My daddy owns the Southern Gentleman, "Fine Apparel for Men," and I have to work there. I don't sell men's underwear like Thelma says. Socks is the nearest thing touching a man's bare skin my daddy lets me sell. He has a very poor opinion of the male population in this town and says no young girl should be discussing a man's private garments. I think he's a little touched in the head on the subject.

"You think I'll catch a social disease? Have a Fruit of the Loom baby?" I say.

"T'ain't funny, McGee!" That's what Rose says, pretending

she's Molly on the radio—you know the show I mean? "Don't talk fresh," she'll call down from the balcony where she alters clothes. Rose is my mom.

Heaven's sake! Look how much I've written and haven't got to the point yet. Well, that's the way it is when I start writing. I travel the long road.

The *point* is the 10 Writing Lessons Course and turning my stories into dollar bills. I figure I'm okay in the writing department, but I don't know beans about selling stories. Yesterday I heard about Sid Brammer killed fighting in Italy. He graduated from Twin Branch High. At his memorial service, Mr. Whiting, the principal, said Sid's ambition was to be a writer like Jesse Stuart, who is highly thought of here in Kentucky—he lives somewhere in the hills. Then Principal Whiting read a poem by Sid called "Love Seeds," about how each of us had seeds of love inside of us and how it was up to each of us to let them grow so finally the whole world would be full of love. It made all the girls cry, including me, and it got me thinking seriously about my future as a writer, seeing how, unlike poor old Sid, I still have one.

So will you send me that first, free lesson? Address it to Twin Branch, Ky. Mr. Gallings at the P.O. knows where to find me. He takes an unnatural interest in my mail. Last week he had a laughing fit because Captain Billy Sparks sent me his *How to Fly an Airplane* manual. I didn't see the joke.

"What happened to the Perfect Partner Dance Studio in Chicago?" he asked, wiping his tears. "You lost interest in learning tap?"

"Two and a half years ago this March," I said, reminding him how long it had been since I cared about tap.

"What about that art school on matchbook covers? I thought for sure you'd win first prize drawing the lady's head in the *Draw Me* contest." Old Gallings can be awful sarcastic when he wants. "And that song you wrote to inspire our fighting boys? You're getting it published in New York, aren't you?"

"I never cared much about songwriting." I lied. I did care until I read where the publishing company wanted me to put up the money!

"So now you're planning your escape in an airplane, huh?" he said, funning me about leaving Twin Branch, which *is* my plan.

"Off like Amelia Earhart," I boasted, "except I don't plan on getting lost."

I wish I could fly some plane to Baltimore, Maryland, where we lived before coming to this hick town. I still might. No one can predict the future. Annie Sturges, the colored lady who keeps house for us, claims she learned how from gypsies camping one summer near Olive Hill. Every morning Annie takes my hand, looking for "vital signs" she claims she's found on everybody except me. One time I took a fountain pen and drew an inky line from my pinkie to my thumb so she'd find something vital, but that only made her mad and she burnt *my* biscuits. "Good thing for you I'm not Bill Farley," I told her.

Send that lesson soon, you hear?

Sincerely yours,
Bobby Lee Pomeroy

7

Bobby Lee Pomeroy
Twin Branch, Kentucky
January 8, 1944

Dear Mr. Pomeroy:

Thank you for your interest in the 10 Writing Lessons
offered by THE GREAT AMERICAN WRITERS
SCHOOL. To be SUCCESSFUL you must have talent,
but you must know how to USE that talent. The climb
up the ladder of SUCCESS is difficult, but if you
follow our instructions YOU can be published in the
FINEST magazines in the country and earn
HUNDREDS of DOLLARS.

For this First Lesson, write about yourself (whatever
you wish) so that our staff of PROFESSIONAL
INSTRUCTORS can evaluate your APTITUDE for
writing. This Lesson is absolutely FREE, but to assure
us of YOUR good intentions, you are advised to send
$10 IN ADVANCE to cover the cost of the 10 Writing
Lessons. (If you fail to have the proper aptitude, your
money will be promptly refunded!)

Send your money today! We at THE GREAT AMERI-
CAN WRITERS SCHOOL are eager to start you
down the ROAD TO SUCCESS!

Yours truly,
HENRY W. BUCKLEY, PRESIDENT
THE GREAT AMERICAN WRITERS SCHOOL
P.O. BOX 140, KOKOMO, INDIANA

Dear Mr. Henry W. Buckley:

I was sure glad to get your nice letter. You made one big mistake though calling me Mister. Don't feel bad because people do that all the time. Blame Rose, my mom, for naming me Bobby Lee with a "y" after a movie star who wasn't even a *star*. She was a starlet! She had her picture taken with Errol Flynn hugging her, for *Silver Screen* or *Photoplay* — Rose can't remember which she was reading in the Johns Hopkins Hospital in Baltimore having me.

Now Rose says she wishes she named me Ginger after Ginger Rogers because when she says, "Bobby Lee this" and "Bobby Lee that," sometimes folks think she's talking about her son, and Rose never wanted a boy.

"Boys go to war," says Rose. "I don't want a Gold Star hanging in my front window like poor Mrs. Brammer."

Rose takes a person's troubles deep in her heart. They don't have to be people she knows like Mrs. Brammer. They can be actors in the movies, play-acting a sad part. Rose loves the movies. She knows what movie stars do for fun, what food they like best, and how they feel about wedding bells and babies. Rose reads the movie mags the way Baptists read the Bible. I tell her she should be on a movie quiz show. She knows facts like Will Rogers's last movie was *In Old Kentucky*, 1935. Heck, she can tell what movie Judy Garland will star in before Judy Garland knows herself.

What Rose doesn't know about is me. "I don't know what goes on in your head, Bobby Lee," she admits. "Your teacher calls you antisocial. Is that the truth?"

The teacher is Miss Amy Watkins, a big snob, who teaches me English grammar and punctuation and is more antisocial than I am. Because I don't want to spend the rest of my life in Twin Branch, married to a dope, with a bunch of freaky kids to raise, people think I'm peculiar. The truth is I don't know one boy in this town worth marrying, except Sid Brammer, and I already wrote what happened to him.

I can't figure what you want to know about me. I'm tall and wear stupid glasses. I actually look older than I am. People are always asking, "Haven't you graduated from high school?" or "When you getting married?"

God almighty! I won't be 15 until May. I don't plan on starting a family yet, though half the girls in this town get started before they graduate. Maybe if I'd been born here I'd be like them and not feel I'm from another planet. How about if I sent a snapshot?

Are you interested in things like my favorite color is orange? My favorite flower is the sunflower. My favorite food is Annie's fried chicken with country gravy, really thick. My favorite subject in school is English from Miss Watkins. Miss Watkins is fierce as a polecat on both grammar and punctuation! She's deeply in love with the Comma, which is probably why she never found a man to marry. If you want to make a good grade from Miss Watkins, use plenty of Commas the way I do. Then you can't miss.

What I don't like about Miss Watkins is the way she grades—hard! Last week she told the class to write a paragraph on what we wanted to do after graduation. I wrote I wanted to be a famous writer like Harriet Beecher Stowe and change the world, or marry a rich English lord, like Our Gal Sunday on the radio. Miss Watkins printed in red ink, "Get serious, Bobby Lee, or you won't amount to a thing!" I *was* serious!

Did I mention my daddy's store is located on the busiest corner in town, Franklin and Winchester, and I'm cashier and chief box maker and wait on customers only when I have to? I pray they aren't hillbillies from around Boone Mountain and Huddy's Creek. They are tanked up on Red Top by 5 o'clock on a Saturday and want to race pickups in front of my daddy's store. Some guys hang on the running board like Keystone Kops out of old movies until Sheriff Farley pulls in his stomach and arrests about a dozen of them.

You'd think they'd learn their lesson, but they don't. My daddy says hillbillies are dumb as tree stumps. I don't think they're dumb. I think they do crazy things because they're bored out of their skulls the way I am! I heard they *beg* to be drafted, but some can't pass the physical test and others are just plain hardship cases and have to stay home to take care of the family.

Twin Branch is dull as knitting needles. There's Keaton's Bowling Alley, the Bluegrass Cafe, where only guys ("No Women Allowed") shoot pool and drink beer, Happy's Skating Rink that Deacon Scully of the First Baptist Church runs strict as a military base, but Twin Branch *does* have two movie theaters. A clean one and a dirty one. The Excellent is the clean one we call the "X." The Capital is where rats run up and down the aisle like they'd paid their admission.

Did you know that Baltimore has about a hundred movie theaters? It's got everything. Once Rose took me to a museum that had enough pictures of naked people lying on the grass to drive every Holy Roller and Baptist in this town plumb crazy. There's a zoo with lions, tigers, monkeys—the works. Did you ever hear of Hutzler's Department Store? My daddy worked there in the men's furnishings department before the Depression laid him off. We'd never have moved here if Daddy hadn't heard about a friend's uncle who was desperate to sell his store. He and Daddy worked out a deal and the uncle is living it up in Florida right now on money Daddy sends him on the first of every month.

Twin Branch doesn't have much besides H. H. Hopkins —"the Triple H," they call it around here—a war plant making things nobody can talk about because "a slip of the lip can sink a ship." Mr. Gallings has a poster hanging in the post office showing a ship full of soldiers sinking in the ocean. There's a big finger pointing straight at *you* as if it's all *your* fault for telling on the Triple H.

"A spy wouldn't be caught dead in this town," I say to Daddy. "Will you stop knocking the town!" Daddy says. "The plant is operating in three shifts. For a change, we have money in the bank."

"Money can't buy happiness," I tell him.

"It already has," he says.

Well, sure—for him.

Did I tell you the SG sells everything for men except shoes? Fredrick's Bootery down the block sells shoes. It used to be called *Fritzie's* Bootery, but with us fighting the Germans, "Fritzie" is pretty unpopular, so Mr. Becker changed it. I feel sorry for him. It's not his fault he sounds like Erich von Stroheim in those Nazi movies. Mr. Becker can't help being born in Germany, but hearing him talk does put people off some. My daddy advised Mr. Becker to show he's as patriotic as the next guy, and now an American flag is flapping outside his store. Having Kate Smith sing "God Bless America" on a loudspeaker was Becker's idea. Folks began to complain her voice was getting on their nerves, and it stopped.

Am I doing the assignment right? I know I have plenty of *aptitude* if you people will give me a chance. I could send a story to prove it. I have good ones about Thelma Thompson. Remember I told you some things about her?

Right now I'm working on a story about Sylvia Weinstock, a new girl in town. Do you want to read it when I'm done? Sylvia's daddy bought the Bon Ton, a ladies store up the block. Her parents are pretty nice, but their daughter is a case. She droops around school like someone just shot her dog.

Let me know if you want to see any of that stuff. Let me know how your installment plan works, too. Writing this assignment has given me the hives. Do I get extra points for *that*? (A joke) Write soon, you hear?

Yours truly,
Bobby Lee Pomeroy

Bobby Lee Pomeroy
Twin Branch, Kentucky
January 28, 1944

Dear Mr. Pomeroy:

Congratulations! Our professional staff read Lesson One with great interest and feels certain you have the kind of *new, fresh, lively talent* that every editor seeks.

We know you must be eager to have Lesson #2: *Defining the Short Story.* You will see how certain elements of a Short Story are fused together by secret techniques; how we have taught aspiring writers to develop creatively and successfully.

We urge you to act. WASTE NO TIME. If it is not ALREADY IN THE MAIL, then send your $10 IMMEDIATELY. Send check or money order.

Remember: this small amount is a BIG INVEST-MENT in your future.

Yours truly,
HENRY W. BUCKLEY, PRESIDENT
THE GREAT AMERICAN WRITERS SCHOOL
P.O. BOX 140, KOKOMO, INDIANA

Twin Branch, Ky.
February 4, 1944

Dear Mr. Henry W. Buckley:

My hands were shaking when I opened your letter. Mr. Gallings said, "Bobby Lee, you lost your color. You going to faint?" To tell the truth, I thought I might. Your letter said *You* have talent. You do mean *me*, don't you? You don't mean a *Mr.* Pomeroy who might have written to you, too? Remember me, Bobby Lee, a girl? I explained it in Lesson #1? I don't care so much about the "Mister" thing, but I wish you'd remembered about the installment plan. The Southern Gentleman has a good installment plan my daddy hired Mr. K. to keep track of.

Mr. K. stands for Mr. James P. Kleykamp. He's been working in the Southern Gentleman since last fall. Before that he was in show business with a mind-reading act he did with his wife, Shirley, until she ran off with a dog trainer when they were playing the Grand Theater in Pikesville, Ky. He said she took their life savings and he had to hitch-hike to get to here. He doesn't like Twin Branch much.

"Too many churches," Mr. K. complains, "not enough sin."

Mr. K. has offered to help me leave town if I want to learn mind reading. He said I could join up with him, be his partner-like—not marry him, of course, but take Shirley's place picking out people's minds in the audience.

"Thanks, but no thanks!" I said. I want out of here, but I don't want to travel with a guy who's old enough to be my daddy. Besides, he's so vain! I hate that! Always checking on himself in the mirror, and if he spots a hangnail on one of his manicured fingers, he operates with clippers as serious as a doctor taking out his own appendix.

Don't get me wrong, I like Mr. K. He's entertaining. "It is a far, far better thing that I do, than I have ever done; it is a far, far better rest that I go to, than I have ever known." He gives that speech like he's Ronald Colman in *A Tale of*

Two Cities. "I'm an ac-*tor*," he recites, phony as a wooden nickel, sweeping the air with his arm, "and all the world is my stage!"

I'm glad I'm not an actor. I'm seriously considering trading places with Sylvia Weinstock, if her folks will have me. Remember I mentioned her? Every afternoon after school you can find Sylvia in a booth in The Rexall Drug Store, drinking cherry smashes and reading *Life* and *Look* magazines from the rack. What a life! Her daddy doesn't make her work in his store!

The only hitch is she's Jewish. You see the newsreels? How Jews are treated in some countries in Europe? How they are shoved in railroad cars and sent to prison camps, even little kids? Then I don't know exactly what happens to them. All I know is watching those newsreels makes me sick to my stomach. Once I thought I saw Sylvia up on the screen, imagining her being scared, holding her coat collar tight around her neck to keep warm, and tears, without any warning, suddenly popped right out of my eyes. Before I could find my handkerchief, the jerk in the projection booth switched the newsreel off and put on a silly cartoon. Woody Woodpecker or Porky Pig was up there dancing, all smiles, happy, and I hadn't time to find my handker-chief even!

I complained to Mr. Kirkpatrick, the manager of the "X." "That was rude," I told him.

"Hell, it's nothing to get excited about, Bobby Lee," Kirkpatrick said. "Jew propaganda is all it is. Don't you go believing everything you see in a newsreel." Standing next to me, he slipped a Clark Bar in my pocket.

Daddy said I should have known better than to reason with Kirkpatrick. He's a loud-mouthed "America Firster" who never wanted us to get in the war. My daddy says Mr. Kirkpatrick has the brains of a flea. I left the Clark Bar on the flea's desk.

I've lost count of the times I tried making friends with Sylvia. She always keeps to herself. I'd like to tell her how sorry I feel for the Jewish people, but when I say, "Hi," I get a smile no bigger than a straight pin. I must be nuts to keep it up. Actually, we don't have much in common. She likes classical music. I like big bands like Tommy Dorsey and Benny Goodman and those guys. Miss Watkins asked Sylvia to play any song she wanted on the piano for assembly. "Your father says you play beautifully," Miss Watkins said, but Sylvia never did.

"Mr. Weinstock doesn't make his daughter work," I tell Daddy about once a week. "No cash. No boxes. No hillbillies."

"Help is hard to find," Daddy argues back, not mean or anything, just acting stubborn like he can be.

"Not for the Bon Ton," I snap right back.

"It's a ladies' store. You can find women to work in a ladies' store. In a men's store you need men," Daddy explains, like he's talking to a moron. "Where do I find men? They are drafted or work at the Triple H," he says. "That's the situation."

"Hire women!"

"Men don't like having women wait on them," my daddy drones on.

"What am I?"

"A little girl," he tells me. "A little girl is O.K."

I'm 5 foot 8 inches and growing and he calls me a *little girl*. When I am 40 years old and tall as a telephone pole, I bet my daddy will still be telling some customer, "My little girl will wait on you."

Well, here I am going on again. Tell your professional staff I said, "Hi," and thanks for counting me in on the Lessons. How about Lesson #2 on credit? With the installment plan we're bound to work out the money situation, so how about it?

Yours in *trust*,
Bobby Lee Pomeroy

Twin Branch, Ky.
February 14, 1944

Dear Mr. Buckley,

Happy Valentine's Day to you! It sure would be nice to hear from you today with Lesson #2. Now that would be a swell Valentine!

I haven't mentioned G.A.W.S. to a soul in town, but Annie Sturges suspects something. This morning at breakfast she said, "Go upstairs and wash your hands."

"I washed them," I told her.

"Hmmm," she said, tracing her pointer finger over my palm, "you're not funning me again, are you?"

"Not so you'd burn my biscuits," I said. "Have you found my future?"

"Something looks different. I think you're running into some kind of luck."

"Good or bad?" I wanted to know right away.

"Can't tell," she said, curling my hand in hers like a cup in a saucer.

"Does it have something to do with getting something special in the mail?" I asked.

"Did you dream of spoons last night?" she said, making me think *she* might be funning *me*. Her dark eyes squinted at the ceiling.

"No," I said, deciding she'd just lost track of my future again. "I dreamed of knives!" I hollered at her.

Annie smiled. "I don't know nothing about knives," she said.

Writing is supposed to be my secret, but folks see my notebooks and know I'm up to something. Most couldn't care less. But Thelma Thompson cares.

Today I watched her grub cigarettes and streetcar fare up at the bank. "It's Miss Snoop, the spy," she said, making some of those old men laugh and look my way. "Now nobody talk about the Triple H or she'll report you to the FBI."

"Why don't you leave the girl alone?" said the one who wears an old cowboy hat tilted back on his head. "She likes you, Thelma."

"Sure she does," said another, rolling a cigarette in one of those little make-your-own contraptions. He wet one side of the paper with his tongue and wrapped the other around what looked like shredded wheat. "You never had a little sister," he said, sticking the nasty thing in his mouth. "Now you got one."

"How do you know?" Thelma said, huffy with him. "You don't know beans about me or my mama."

"Not your mama, honey," said another old guy hairy as a grizzly, "but I knew your daddy before he run off. He wasn't much of a family man. Wasn't home long enough to make more than one baby."

"That's all you know!" Thelma said and gave him the evil eye. He kind of laughed and tapped her shoulder with his cob pipe like he didn't mean her any harm.

I was standing there, writing it all down as I heard it, when Thelma grabbed for my pen. Lucky I dodged and ran off. I heard one of the men say, "Isn't she cute when she's mad?" meaning Thelma, of course, and then they all began to laugh.

God almighty! Grown men! Old Thelma had whittled them down to schoolboys. She doesn't work *or* go to school, but she can spark the men, all right, except for Mr. K. Mr. K. hadn't been in town a week before he asked me, "Who is that little tramp?"

"You mean Thelma Thompson? She's no tramp. She lives right here in Twin Branch," I said.

"Pardon me," he said with a funny smile.

I knew what he meant, but I don't much like people picking on Thelma. Why wouldn't guys flock around her, as good-looking as she is? She's blond and has wicked green eyes and she's very developed, if you know what I mean. She's a sight prettier and smarter than most girls in this town you see wandering like sleepwalkers through the Five and Dime, smearing Tangee lipstick on the back of their hands and congregating at the candy cases and calling boys "cannon fodder" like it's a big joke. If I were a guy, it would send shivers down my spine. Do those girls care? All they care about is getting a date for jukebox Saturday night.

My daddy would die of natural causes if I had a date any day of the week. Daddy says the males around here have *one* thing on their minds.

"What's that?" I'll ask him, opening my eyes big as supper plates. I'm half playing because, I'll be truthful with you, I don't know much about the *thing*. I mean I don't have any actual experience. "Talk to your mother," Daddy says, but Rose and I can't talk about personal things. I wish we were close. When I was little, I found this anatomy book in the library that showed what goes where with *diagrams*. At first I thought they were silly, but then I got kind of sick in my stomach. Look—let's just forget I brought up the subject, O.K.?

I'd really appreciate you digging out my letter from that big pile on your desk. It says I'm waiting on you for Lesson #2, asking you to trust me. I won't let you down.

Impatiently yours,
Bobby Lee Pomeroy

Bobby Lee Pomeroy
Twin Branch, Kentucky
February 19, 1944

Dear Mr. Pomeroy:

Congratulations! Our professional staff read Lesson One with great interest and feel certain you have the

kind of *new, fresh, lively talent* that every editor seeks.

We know you must be eager to have Lesson #2: *Defining the Short Story*. You will see how certain elements of a Short Story are fused together by secret techniques; how we have taught aspiring writers to develop creatively and successfully.

We urge you to act. WASTE NO TIME. If it is not ALREADY IN THE MAIL, then send your $10 IMMEDIATELY. Send check or money order.

Remember: this small amount is a BIG INVESTMENT in your future.

Yours truly,
HENRY W. BUCKLEY, PRESIDENT
THE GREAT AMERICAN WRITERS SCHOOL
P.O. BOX 140, KOKOMO, INDIANA

Twin Branch, Ky.
February 26, 1944

Dear Mr. Buckley,

Today I received your letter congratulating me a second time! I've been congratulated twice! 2 times. What about Lesson #2? I'm worried you changed your mind about me. You haven't, have you?

I'm writing this from the SG after a rush trip to Rexall's. On the radio Rose keeps on the sewing machine table, she heard Jimmy Fiddler mention how Rita Hayworth gave

Movieland a scoop on her latest romance, and I knew Rose wouldn't be able to concentrate on shortening a pair of green corduroys until she had that magazine in her hand. Rose has this obsession with Rita Hayworth. Don't ask me why. It's a fact of life. So I went to Rexall's to get the magazine for her.

As soon as I walked in the door, I spotted Sylvia Weinstock. Reading a book. Hunkered down in her favorite booth with a cherry smash.

"Hi," I said like I always do, and she didn't say, "Hi," back like she always doesn't.

She took a ladylike sip of the red stuff, her eyes fixed, straying neither left nor right of that book.

It's funny, but I have a theory Sylvia tries to be friendly. I mean I don't feel that she hates me. Something holds her back, like she thinks I might have B.O. (body odor) or halitosis (bad breath) or something more dangerous. O.K., so I took an empty stool at the counter and ordered a cherry smash myself when who should come waltzing in and sit right down *next* to me? Thelma Thompson! She ordered a Coke, not looking my way, unrolling a comic book on the counter so everybody could see what a deep thinker she was.

"You like Captain America?" I asked, casually, so I wouldn't get my head chopped off.

"I'm *reading* Captain America, ain't I?"

I hate it when she barks like a seal. She flipped pages without reading a word, then stopped at an advertisement that jumped off the page: YOU CAN MAKE $25 — $50 — $100 SELLING CHRISTMAS CARDS!

"Jeepers creepers! Mind if I look at that?" I said.

"Keep it if you want." She slid the comic over, showing off her Cutex Dragon Lady red nail polish. "I got no need for it."

"I do! I need cash. *Cash* is what I need," I repeated, hoping she'd ask why, but she didn't. "Do you think I could earn $100 in a hurry?"

"Selling Christmas cards in March?" Thelma started in laughing. "You're crazy," she said.

I'd never seen Thelma laugh. She has real pretty teeth.

"I need the money now," I went on, but she definitely wasn't interested in having a heart-to-heart.

"When is your birthday?" Thelma suddenly screwed up her eyes like I was a needle she was threading.

"May 5th."

"Taurus," she said. "Stubborn as a bull. No wonder I can't get rid of you. That's why you got money on your mind. Taurus people are like that."

"You believe that horoscope stuff?"

"Don't know why you'd need money," she said, ignoring my question. "Your daddy must be rich owning a store. Ask your daddy for the money, why don't you?"

"I can't. It's a secret."

When I said that, her face changed to an evil smile. "I love secrets," she said, like I knew the combination to Fort Knox. "Tell me. I won't tell." I was ready to spill the beans about G.A.W.S. when Doc Bowie came out from the pharmacy and sat on the stool next to Thelma. He put his hand on her shoulder that she shook loose. "How's your mother, Thelma?" Doc Bowie said, taking no offense. "She's doing all right," she muttered through lips tight as a zipper.

"Still in bed?" Doc asked. "Taking her pills, is she?"

"Yeah, she's still in bed, taking pills."

"That's too bad," Doc Bowie said. "Well, tell her I asked for her."

Then the front door burst open and Thelma's friend with the cowboy hat stuck his head in. "Thelma!" he yelled. "I thought you were getting me coffee! What the hell do you think you're doing?"

"Hold your horses, Emory. It's coming."

"When? Tomorrow?"

Doc Bowie hollered, "You're making a damn draft."

"Hurry it up," Emory said and left, but Thelma didn't hurry. She combed her hair and put on lipstick before she asked for coffee to go.

"See you around," she said, winking like she'd get my secret another time, and off she went on those spiky heels.

That's the first I'd heard about Thelma's mom in bed. I asked Doc what was the matter with her.

"Poverty" was all he would tell me.

"I didn't know you took pills for that," I grumbled.

So I don't know if the woman is crippled or blind or both. With no husband, no family, I guess only Thelma takes care of her, but it's hard imagining Thelma carrying bedpans and wiping sweat off a person's face the way nurses do in the movies. I can imagine Thelma flirting with Dr. Kildare when he comes by to check on her mom, but that's as far as I can stretch for Nurse Thelma.

I drank another cherry smash and thought I'd give Sylvia another chance. "What are you reading, kiddo?" I flipped like I was Red Skelton or some comedian on the radio.

Sylvia didn't bat an eyelash.

My curiosity was busting my sides. I practically fell in her lap trying to read the title of the book she was holding on to for dear life.

I read it, all right, and backed off in a hurry! You want to know why?

Sylvia was reading a prayer book! Honest— the words were printed on a black leathery cover.

Why would a person pray in a drug store? You tell me! Twin Branch must have 20 churches on Franklin Street alone. You can't miss them. Standing there, with my mouth open, I knew one good thing—I finally had her attention.

"Did I disturb you?" I faked an apology. "Hope you didn't lose your place in your book. Looks very interesting, all right," I rambled on, getting a chill from her icy stare. "Don't know much about religion. Any kind of religion. Maybe you could help me out. What do you say?"

Of course, the Great Stone Face made no reply, so I made a beeline for the magazine rack and bought Rose her copy of *Movieland* and left. I sensed Sylvia's cold eyes following me out the door, her sharp claws scratching at my back.

"Isn't she cute?" Rose asked, admiring Dorothy Lamour wrapped in her sarong on the cover of the movie mag.

"Cute as a button," I said, doing the imitation of Donald Duck Rose hates. Rose ignored me. Her eyes didn't flicker.

This must have been my day to be ignored. Passed over. It's all so *boring*!

Could I ask you a serious question and get an honest answer? Do you think I'm conceited? The word is out at school that I am. Would you help me out and tell me what you think? I need some help from somebody. Do you see the dollar bill stuck to this paper? It's my first payment to G.A.W.S. I was saving for the Precious Waterman Fountain Pen, but like you said, G.A.W.S. is an *investment* in my future and I'd better get a move on—especially after yesterday. I found an old street map of Baltimore in the sideboard, and, when I closed my eyes and pointed my finger, where do you think I landed? On *Liberty Road*!

Annie says that's a vital sign. Get it? Liberty like in *Liberty* magazine, where I found your advertisement. Liberty like in freedom and freedom like in free of men's socks, ties, belts, shirts, hats, gloves, overalls, mackinaws— and of hillbillies!

Write soon! Please!

Pining for Lesson #2!
Bobby Lee Pomeroy

Bobby Lee Pomeroy
Twin Branch, Kentucky
March 1, 1944

Dear Miss Pomeroy:

As a member of the 10 Writing Lessons Course, *you* are now eligible to receive a copy of WRITERS GUIDE for the small amount of only $1.00. That's right! Only $1.00! SPECIAL *for members only*.

WRITERS GUIDE tells you everything you *need* to know to *sell* your creative efforts. You'll read about editors, publishers, and famous writers with *tips*!

Only WRITERS GUIDE gives this VALUABLE information on magazines, newspapers, and book publishers across the country—*with addresses*.

You can't *afford* to miss this one-time offer! SEND $1.00 by money order today. Let WRITERS GUIDE guide you down the PATH OF SUCCESS!

Yours truly,
SUSAN BUCKLEY, EDITOR
WRITERS GUIDE
THE GREAT AMERICAN WRITERS SCHOOL
P.O. BOX 140, KOKOMO, INDIANA

Twin Branch, Ky.
March 7, 1944

Dear Miss Susan Buckley, Editor:

If you believe in fate, you'll know how I felt when I read your letter. I'm writing a special story, and here you come along, a female I can confide in, offering me a helping hand. *Writers Guide* sounds like just the ticket for a person living in the sticks the way I do.

The story is absolutely *true*. I'll swear to it.

I was walking up Franklin Street to get coffee for my daddy, who was busy with a customer needing a blue serge suit for his wedding. I was turning the corner to Burle Street when a boy jumped off a Blue Ribbon bus parked at the depot and knocked me off my feet. I landed on Mr. Burgess, one of the regulars, sleeping on the waiting bench.

"I'm sorry," the boy apologized to the both of us. "I'm really sorry." Mr. Burgess took a big swing at him, missing by a mile and making a terrible ruckus. I tell you, I was so embarrassed I about died.

When the commotion died down, I took a long look at the guy causing the trouble. He was a redhead, taller than me, thank heavens, and real good-looking. In case you don't know, I work in the Southern Gentleman, my daddy's store, so I know a thing or two about sizing up men. Offhand I'd say he wore a size 15 shirt, number 3 sleeve, 30" waist, not including the leather belt with the silver buckle in the shape of a horseshoe. I wouldn't know about his inseam, not wanting to stare.

"I guess I didn't hurt you none," the redhead said to me. "Didn't even mess up that pretty black hair." I must have blushed. My cheeks felt on fire.

"Yes, ma'am," he went on, all smiles. "You look fine to me."

"Hillbilly!" I said, like it was an incurable disease, and ran off, huffing and puffing, like I didn't care a fig about him. But my heart was fluttering like paper caught in an electric fan.

"Where's my coffee?" Daddy wanted to know.

"I forgot it!" I'd run so fast I plumb forgot my errand, but I hadn't outrun the redhead because he was standing in the doorway, grinning and motioning for me to come outside. When Daddy saw him, he took him for a customer and asked him what he wanted to buy. Red spoke right up, "Her! How much?" he said.

Well, I thought my heart would pop out of my mouth.

My daddy got so mad, he hollered, "Get away from here before I call the sheriff!"

Red vanished like he'd been vaporized.

"Why did you holler at him?" I said.

"Do you know that boy?" Daddy asked.

"He looked familiar," I lied.

"From where?"

I hate when my daddy gets suspicious. I've never given him any reason to be — hardly any.

"I think he used to go to the high school," I said, scratching my head like I was thinking hard on the matter.

"Don't let me see him around here again," Daddy said. "I mean it, Bobby Lee." My daddy does, too.

I wished Daddy hadn't been so rude. It's the way he is when it comes to me and boys. I suspect Daddy plans to lock me up in the closet and throw away the key. His plan is for me to be an old maid, selling Big Ben overalls at the Southern Gentleman the rest of my life. What kind of future is that for a writer?

You know what's so good about writing? I can say anything that pops in my head. I can have Red be a hero like Leslie Howard in *The Scarlet Pimpernel* (I love Leslie Howard!) or a GI Joe who's ready to be shipped overseas and searching for a someone he can open his heart to. Someone like me.

I know it sounds strange, but I feel in my bones you and I are going to be friends. That's why I'm asking you to send *Writers Guide* on credit. I have an installment plan in the works with Henry W. Buckley. (Is he your husband or daddy?) Well, you guys must have a plan because I sent Mr. Buckley a dollar and he never sent it back.

By the way, I *love* the name Susan. I told Rose (my mom) I wished she had named me Susan. She should have, liking Susan Hayward the way she does, but not as much as she likes Rita Hayworth, but we can go into all that another time.

Hopefully yours,
Bobby Lee Pomeroy

Twin Branch, Ky.
March 11, 1944

Dear Miss Susan Buckley,

Remember the redhead I wrote about? The boy on the Blue Ribbon bus? I found out his name is Dempsey Fanin and he's *not* a hillbilly. He came by again last week while daddy was playing pool at the Bluegrass Cafe and invited me for a Coke. I knew I shouldn't leave the SG, but I followed him into Rexall's anyhow.

I was curious about his name. "Were you named for Jack Dempsey the prizefighter?" I asked him.

"People are always asking," he said, like he was tired of hearing it. "It was my mother's name before she married my daddy," he said. "My given name is Lyle, but nobody calls me that."

Dempsey comes from a farm near Lexington, Ky. His mom died when he was a little kid and he lives on a horse farm with his daddy. He's 18 years old and graduated last month in one of those hurry-up programs so boys can have their diploma before they are drafted into the armed forces. His daddy wanted him to get deferred and go to the University of Kentucky, but he already signed up with the Air Force.

You are interested in this, aren't you? I sure am, for the story, you know. I was glad he didn't ask how old I was. I'd have lied. He probably thinks I'm his age on account of me being tall and wearing glasses. We talked mostly about horses. I don't know a darn thing about horses.

"You never been on a horse?" Dempsey asked me, like, "You never been to the *moon*?"

"Well, once in Baltimore at Carlin's Amusement Park I rode one on the carousel," I said to be funny. He didn't laugh.

"I have my own horse. He's a 3-year-old named General Eisenhower."

"Come on! Eisenhower? You're kidding." I almost laughed in his face. I'm glad I didn't, because Dempsey takes the generals very seriously. He can name every general fighting on our side of the war. On his bedroom wall he has a world map so he can follow GIs wherever the generals send them.

"You stick little colored pins on the map?" I said, acting cute.

"Sure do," he said.

"Sounds like fun." Still acting cute.

"I wouldn't call it fun. When the invasion comes, it'll be hard keeping up."

"What invasion?" I asked, but I really did know. Honest.

"The invasion of Europe!" he said. "GIs are in England

right now waiting for a signal from General Eisenhower."

"Your horse?" I was funning again, edgy though, thinking Daddy might come searching for me.

"No, General *Ike* Eisenhower!" Dempsey snapped at me. Well, you know what people say about redheads — how hotheaded they can be.

"I'm sorry. I know who he is." My voice was calmer than I felt deep inside. My eyes were glued to the door.

"What about you, Bobby Lee?" he asked. "What are you interested in?"

I wasn't about to mention G.A.W.S. or Harriet Beecher Stowe. If we get close, I might. By this time, I'd been gone from the SG for an hour. I truly, actually, could see my Daddy crash straight through the glass door when he saw me with Dempsey.

"Look, I've got to run," I said, gulping the last of my third Coke. "I'm really sorry."

"I'll walk you back," Dempsey said.

"You'd better not," I warned him, but he went with me out to the street and there was Thelma Thompson standing at the curb.

"Hi, Miss Snoop," she said loud, in her rude way. Dempsey didn't take notice. He and Thelma were busy sizing each other up and down. Thelma was wearing her Saturday Night Special and flashing the smile that showed off her good teeth. Right away I could see she thought he was good-looking.

I hated to leave them together, but I was thinking Daddy would kill me if he caught me with Dempsey. Halfway down the block I turned to see Thelma wiggling, with her hands on her hips. "Bette Davis vamping Leslie Howard. *Of Human Bondage*," I said, disgusted, remembering the scene. "I should have my head examined for introducing those two."

As soon as I walked in, Daddy gave me a dirty look and a bundle of pants to take up to the balcony where Rose was chalking a coat sleeve.

"Errol Flynn has a new girlfriend," Rose said, really pissed off about it.

"Who cares?" I said.

"He's driving himself to an early grave." Rose had scissors, snipping along chalk lines.

"Who cares?"

"He was picked up by the police for drunkenness on Hollywood Boulevard." The scissors opened wide and sliced a piece of gray tweed. I picked the cloth up from the floor and handed it to her.

"I hope they put him in jail for life," I said, miserable at the thought of what could be happening in front of Rexall's.

I left Rose on the balcony deciding where the swatch of gray material belonged. I knew, but didn't say. She'd made a big mistake on that sleeve.

It's late. I've waited on a hundred hillbillies. Dempsey hasn't passed. Neither has Thelma. My daddy has his eye on me sharp as a gun sight, so I can't leave to look for them.

You might not be interested in this, but I was busting to tell somebody and picked you because you are female and understand writers.

Your friend (say you are),
Bobby Lee Pomeroy

Bobby Lee Pomeroy
Twin Branch, Kentucky
March 15, 1944

Dear Miss Pomeroy:

**The staff at THE GREAT AMERICAN WRITERS
SCHOOL has approved your receiving this copy of
WRITERS GUIDE *with the understanding* that you
recognize your obligation to pay *in full* for the 10
Writing Lessons Course *and* WRITERS GUIDE on
receipt of the book.**

The total amount: $11.00.

**We trust you will keep in mind the valuable bene-
fits we offer you as we guide you—an aspiring
writer—down the PATH TO SUCCESS! Please
send $11.00 check or money order for full payment
to the School today.**

Yours truly,
SUSAN BUCKLEY, EDITOR
WRITERS GUIDE
THE GREAT AMERICAN WRITERS SCHOOL
P.O. BOX 140, KOKOMO, INDIANA

Twin Branch, Ky.
March 20, 1944

Dear Miss Buckley,

You are a dream come true! *Writers Guide* is everything
you said. I love it! I carry it with me—it's my good luck
charm. Last night I slept with it! Crazy, huh?

I was tempted to show it off to Sylvia Weinstock, who actually mumbled a "hello" to me today—the first mumble I've had—but Thelma Thompson scooted into the empty booth behind Sylvia's, so I put Sylvia's mumble on the back burner and invited myself to sit with Thelma.

"I hate walking," Thelma began to whine as soon as I sat down. "I hate Pollard Road. Look at my shoes, will you? One holy mess. Hey," she said, looking at me for the first time, "where's the farm boy? He been around?"

"What farm boy?" I stood *Writers Guide* on end in front of her.

"You know better than play games with me, Bobby Lee."

I did know better. I said, "Dempsey?"

"That his name?" She pretended surprise, not fooling me. "Suppose he's named for the prizefighter?"

"No" was all I'd tell her. I pushed the book forward.

"He's cute," she said, ignoring the book.

"You think so? You don't have a crush on him, do you?" I said, holding my breath.

"Naw, he's too young. I'm not robbing no cradle." She gave me a little crooked smile I'd never seen. It was almost friendly.

"He's old enough to join the Air Force," I said, knowing too late I'd said too much.

Thelma smiled at that. "He should get deferred like the guys around here who work at the Triple H. Emory could get him a job if he wanted. Making things for the war, a person earns good money."

"Speaking of money," I said and held *Writers Guide* right up to her eyes, "see what I got in the mail."

Thelma took the book from me and opened it to Chapter #9: *Preparing to Sell*. "You plan to sell stuff you write about me?"

"Maybe," I said.

"Do I get any money?"

"Not unless you want to help with the writing," I said.

"Now, that'll be the day!" She let the book fall on the table with a thud. "You don't catch me spying on people, creeping around the way you do. No, ma'am. Wouldn't turn down an offer to be an actress, though."

"Take the C&O north. There are plenty of jobs for actresses in Baltimore. I hear they are crying for actresses in Baltimore," I lied.

"No, dummy, I mean in the *movies*," she said. "How about me in one of those long white evening gowns you see actresses wear. Or me in a bathing suit. I could wear a sarong—anything you name, I look good in."

There was no doubt in my mind that Thelma was ready to go to hell in a basket to get in the movies.

"Why don't you enter a movie contest?" I said.

"I don't know anything about contests."

"Ask my mom," I said. "She can tell you everything you want to know."

Thelma chewed on her lip, thinking and nodding her head. "That's not such a bad idea, Bobby Lee," she said. "Emory says I'm prettier than Betty Grable, and all the GIs have her picture stuck up."

"Do you like to listen to Harry James? Her husband," I informed her in case she didn't know. "I'm more of a Glenn Miller fan myself, but I've got a bunch of Harry James records you can listen to any time you want." I could just picture Thelma and me, sprawled on my bed, munching Annie's peanut-butter cookies, listening to "I Cried for You" on the record player. I kind of liked the picture, but it did make me laugh.

"What's so funny?" Thelma said. "You laughing at me?"

"No. It's not you. I'm feeling good," I said. "I've made a new friend and she sent me this book." Again I showed her the book you sent and told her, "This is going to change my life."

"Hell's fire," Thelma said in her old rough voice. "Who am I kidding? I got no life. I'm not going to get one till Mama gets out of bed and tends to herself, and she's not about to do that."

"Why is your mom in bed, Thelma? Is she crippled? Did she break her leg? Look," I said, seeing her green eyes flash, "you know I'm a curious person. I can't help asking questions. I was born that way."

I went on excusing myself, but she paid no attention to me. She left without ever ordering. I watched her through the window as she crossed the street to where the old guys were leaning against the side of the bank. Seeing her long blond hair flip from side to side, I knew for sure if a movie scout took a turn off the highway into town, he'd leap out of his car to sign her up. He'd hand her a contract and say, "Name your price, babe," and if it only covered the price of a new pair of shoes, I'd tell her to take it. Sooner or later she's bound to break a leg in that pair she's wearing. I doubt there's much call for a one-legged actress, no matter how good-looking.

At supper my daddy wanted to talk about trousers without cuffs. The newspaper said the government ordered "no cuffs" to save material for soldiers' uniforms. Daddy says trousers look terrible with no cuff. "Skimpy," he says. "Cheap."

I wasn't especially interested in this line of conversation and began to skip through my *Writers Guide*. I'd reached Chapter #4: *Romance: Pulp or Slick?* when I noticed Daddy looking from me to the *Guide* opened on my lap. It was a strong hint to close it. I was hoping he'd ask what I was reading, but he didn't. "Don't read at the table" was all he said.

Putting the book on the floor, I made a mental note to write about a cold-hearted father who didn't give a fig about his daughter being a famous writer and, in the end, she turned out better than Harriet Beecher Stowe! (Did you read *Uncle Tom's Cabin*? It's hard going. I tried, is all I can say.)

Believe it or not, getting riled up at Daddy did lift my spirits some. They'd been dragging after Thelma walked out on me the way she did.

I don't know one reason why I should care about that girl or her mom! What's it to me if her mom stays in bed the rest of her life? What do I care if Thelma wants to be a movie star? Every girl in America wants to be a movie star! If Harriet Beecher Stowe were alive today, *she'd* want to be a movie star and we'd still have slavery!

Well, thank you for reading this and thank you for the book. I appreciate you trusting me the way you do. Annie Sturges said my luck was changing, and this time she turned out to be right. You sending the book was a vital sign. I hope you write me.

Grateful forever,
Bobby Lee

P.S. If you want to buy Christmas cards, let me know. Only 25 cents for a box of 15 cards. Pictures of the Baby Jesus or Christmas trees in the snow. Take your pick. Your credit is good with me.

Twin Branch, Ky.
April 11, 1944

Dear Miss Buckley,

I've been saying G.A.W.S. is my secret, and then I go and let the cat out of the bag. Now Miss Watkins knows. I was tricked into telling her.

This morning she was saying how I must have been eating Mexican jumping beans for breakfast instead of corn flakes — a big joke, making everyone in class laugh. I didn't know what she was talking about — she's queer sometimes.

"Why do you fidget so? Can't you sit still?" she asked me.

"I'm still!" I told her and folded my hands on top of my desk with some kids still snickering.

"I'm glad to see you are because, Bobby Lee, you've been making me nervous. What is your problem? You want to talk about it?" Without waiting for my answer, which would have been "No," she said, "See me after school."

So I stayed after school and confessed how staking out the post office every day, hoping to hear from you, had me jittery and short-tempered. I can't sleep. I've lost my appetite. I'm bored up to my eyeballs with my life!

"Let me understand this," Miss Watkins said sternly. "You're having this fit because you haven't heard from a classified ad you answered?"

"Don't you see? I'm planning my future like you said. I'm planning to be a famous writer. The Great American Writers School can teach me the tricks of the trade."

I waited for her to congratulate me, seeing how I'd put my ambition plan into action. She didn't. She closed her eyes, breathed real deep, in sort of a trance, the way she is explaining transitive and intransitive verbs.

"No, no, no, Bobby Lee, no," she said, and added a few more "no"s for good measure. "There are no tricks to being a writer. Writing — good writing — is not trickery. You understand me?"

She stared hard into my eyes and I nodded my head, even though I didn't understand. "I am talking about literature. Don't waste your life on anything else. If you form the habit of reading literature, you will eventually recognize the artistry of storytelling. You will recognize good writing as the *art* it is and find the essentials for yourself."

What *essentials*? I didn't know what she was talking about. "I read," I said, weakly.

"You read trashy detective magazines. I've seen them tucked under your arm. You read movie magazines."

"I buy them for Rose. My mother. I only look at the pictures."

"You read confession and pulp magazines. Is that the kind of writer you wish to be?"

"I don't know," I said.

"I'm referring to books by distinguished writers who made their reputation by writing good books. Poe, Dickens, Faulkner, Twain, Fitzgerald, many others. Read their books. Study them. You don't need $10 of worthless lessons for something you can learn yourself *if*, Bobby Lee, *if* you're serious and willing to work."

You see what I've let myself in for? I know you and G.A.W.S. can teach me everything I need to know, but Miss Watkins has magic powers over a person's mind. A shiver went down my spine when she unlocked the glass doors to her private bookcase behind her desk. "Watkins's Law," she once told my class, was never to loan any of her books, but there she was, handing me a book with a green leather cover and gold letters spelling "O. Henry." I almost died.

"Here are stories to read and study," she said, sounding almost cheerful. "Think about the characters. Who they are. What they do. Why they do what they do. What is the story the writer wishes to tell?"

Then, using her teacher voice again, she said, "Do not turn down the corners of the pages and do not crack the spine of the binding. Return it when you have finished, and if I decide you are worthy, I will bring you other books from home."

At that, I considered making a run for the door. Miss Watkins's daddy was a professor at the University of Kentucky, and when he died, he left her a house full of books. People say there's more books in her library than in the public library the WPA built in 1936. If I read all those books, I won't have *time* to write!

Another thing—Miss Watkins told me I had to learn *Latin*. Now, do I?

"You can't be a writer without a knowledge of Latin," she said.

"Nobody speaks Latin," I argued, weak as a flat tire.

"My dear," she said, *not* nicely, "everybody speaks Latin!"

I don't want to learn Latin, but there's no way to say no to Miss Watkins. If there is, I haven't found it.

Well, before I forget it—Thelma Thompson is entering a movie contest! Rose found one in *Movieland*. The rules ask for Thelma's picture and for her to write an essay: "Why I want to be a movie star." Thelma can't write worth dirt, so guess who she begged to do it for her? Guess who said she would (and should have her head examined)? I knew you'd guess right both times.

Fidus, (Latin)
Bobby Lee

P.S. Did you know O. Henry's real name was William Sydney Porter? How do you suppose writers get good, phony names like that? From the telephone book?

Twin Branch, Ky.
April 17, 1944

Dear Susan,

How are you? Why don't you drop me a line sometime, O.K.? How's Mr. Buckley? What's happening? Shouldn't I be getting a Lesson or something in the mail?

I'm ready to level with you, Sue. I don't write 5 and sometimes 6 stories in a day. What I write is not exactly a story. I don't know what to call it. I keep *track* of people. It gives me something to do and think about. When I write in my notebooks, people look at me, do you know what I mean? I'm not just vapor floating in the air. Well, I'll explain another time. I just wanted you to know that the Lessons are important to me.

This week Thelma and I worked on the movie contest I told you about. Tomorrow Thelma's friend Emory is driving her over to the Del Mar Photography Studio in Ashland and he's paying for the pictures of her for the contest.

Thelma is lucky to have a friend like Emory. They are quite comical together. She'll whine, "Did you see the Evening in Paris perfume set in Rexall's window?" He knows what's coming next, and sure enough Thelma says, "Can I have it for a treat?"

Well, he'll go right in and buy it for her, nice as you please. He's got a temper, though. "Where you been?" he'll snap at her in front of everybody and their uncle. "Did you pick up my clothes from the cleaners like I told you?" Emory lives at home with his mother, same as Thelma does with hers, only his mother doesn't spend her days and nights in bed. Emory's mother works at the Triple H.

Thelma was grumbling today. "If Mama would get out of bed, I could get me a steady job," she said. "Mama's been in bed so long she thinks she's cripple, but she's not cripple."

Doc Bowie told me the pills he gives Thelma's mom are nothing but candy drops. I asked why he gave them to her.

He said he'd been doing it for so long, he'd forgotten. He doesn't charge her.

"Can't you make your mom get out of bed?" I said to Thelma.

"You mean set the house on fire or something like that?"

"If you have to. At least, break up the bed."

You might think that was a cruel thing to say about a sick person, but my mind wasn't exactly on Thelma's problems. In fact, that's one reason I'm writing to you today.

Don't be mad, you hear? I've been sneaking out of the SG regular to meet Dempsey Fanin. I tell my daddy I'm running errands for Rose, but I'm not. I'm meeting Dempsey. Dempsey is the first boy I've ever had a crush on. I do, you know. I greatly admired Sid Brammer, but I never had goose pimples thinking about Sid, dead or alive, the way I have thinking about Dempsey. When we're together, all we do is drink Cokes and talk about the war. We never do anything romantic like hold hands or wink.

"When I get into the Air Force, I'm going to be the Number 1 Ace," Dempsey told me. "People are going to talk about me the way they talk about Eddie Rickenbacker and Dick Bong. Here I come," he said, pushing imaginary buttons and yanking on a pretend stick like John Wayne in *Flying Tigers*. "Watch my smoke, Nazis!" he hollered right there in the drug store. "I'm coming to get you!" He didn't care if people were looking—and they were.

"You mean the Germans, right?" I said. Of course, I know the Nazis are Germans, but you'd be surprised how hard it is to think of things to say when Dempsey gets riled up like that.

"They want to own the whole world and they'll kill you if you get in their way," Dempsey said. "Do you know they round up people like cattle, hundreds of them, and shoot them down, hundreds at a time? Well, that's what you hear."

"*The March of Time* showed it. At the 'X.' Last Wednesday."

"Did it show people walking to labor camps, and if they weren't in a straight line, they'd be shot?"

"You mean people like the Jews?" I said to show I knew something. "There's a Jewish family living right here in Twin Branch." I turned to point out Sylvia, but wouldn't you know she wouldn't be in her booth when I wanted her to be?

"Well," I said, "so you're ready to go. Not waiting to be drafted, huh? Enlisted, have you?"

"My dad wants me to say I'm needed on the farm. I wouldn't have to go then. I told him I was ready to serve my country. I was proud to be fighting for the good old red, white, and blue!"

I listened with a nice smile, but hoping the Air Force turns him down—says he's 4-F and can't go. Dempsey would die if he knew I wrote you that. He hasn't a clue how dear I think he is. He treats me like a sister. I don't want to be his sister. How do I *tell* him that? How do I come straight out and say, "I'm nuts about you, Dempsey," without being fresh? Should I send for one of those love potions advertised in the magazines? What do you think? It works, it says, without talking.

You can see why it's hard to concentrate on Thelma's problem with her mama when I have problems of my own.

Anyhow I'm stuck on the essay. It's not the actual writing. I don't understand why Thelma wants to be in the movies.

"Tell them I want to catch me a rich Hollywood guy," Thelma tells me. Now, that wouldn't win a free balloon, would it?

In *Winesburg, Ohio* by Sherwood Anderson (Miss Watkins loaned it to me) this man says, "I am a lover and have not found my thing to love."

Isn't that the saddest thing you ever read? Doesn't it hurt your heart?

What if I wrote that *Hollywood* was Thelma's thing to love? I could write how nothing else mattered to her as much as going to Hollywood and being in the movies.

There's only one trouble in doing that—I have the suspicion Thelma's thing is *Dempsey*!

I can't shake it.

But—if we win the contest, I won't have to worry. She'd be gone. Out of sight.

I wish I could send Miss Watkins with her. Those "books from home" she's bringing me keep me reading day and night and night and day. I said I had a personal interest in the war (my interest being Dempsey) and now I have a load of war books. *The Red Badge of Courage* by Stephen Crane isn't even about Nazis. It takes place in the *American Civil War*. It's good to read, all right. Some scary scenes dig into your mind, like when the soldier, Henry, has the vision of "black columns of enemy troops disappearing on the brow of a hill like two serpents crawling from the cavern of night."

Reading that made my skin crawl.

I've got to go now, but I'd appreciate any special advice you have for winning a trip for Thelma to Hollywood. Any little hint.

Do you suppose your daddy lost my address? Will Lesson #2 be traveling through space soon, coming my way?

Adsum, (Latin for "I am here"—waiting.)
Bobby Lee

Twin Branch, Ky.
April 22, 1944

Dear Susan,

Here's the latest scoop on my life—last Thursday I walked the 6 miles from the SG to Pollard Road where Thelma lives. I'd never walked that part of town before, mostly because it's no nature walk, believe me. Pollard Road is nothing but dirt and rocks. No sidewalks in sight. Old cars missing half their guts make one long line of junk on the road. The houses aren't in much better shape. Porches look ready to cave in under loads of old washing machines, tacky furniture, broken toys—you name it.

The Thompson house was the last one before reaching a field of tin and trash you could rightly call a dump. Seeing no doorbell, I knocked, and after a long while Thelma appeared dressed in a blue, beat-up cotton robe. Without her spiky heels, heck, she's shorter than me.

"What are you doing *here?*" Thelma kind of screamed.

"I just happened to be passing on my way to Warner Brothers Studios. I hear Paramount is over the hill." She frowned and stood her ground with one arm blocking the doorway. "Look, I'd have telephoned if you had one. I brought you the essay for the contest."

"You could have given it to Emory like I told you," she said.

"I needed the exercise. Fresh air. Sunshine. My daddy was saying today how I was looking pale and puny. He said how I needed to get out in the country for my health, so here I am, doing what my daddy told me."

Thelma thought for a minute, sucking her thumb like a little kid. I supposed she was considering whether or not to invite me in. Finally, she did.

Inside, there wasn't much to see. A lumpy brown sofa in one corner, a round table surrounded by wooden chairs that didn't match. On the table was the stack of movie magazines Rose had given her. Next to the magazines was an ashtray full of smelly cigarette butts. Thelma picked up one butt, still smoking, and stuck it in her mouth.

"You shouldn't smoke so much."

"A pack a day," Thelma boasted. "Can't live without my Luckies."

"My daddy smokes Camels. Four packs a day, then he coughs all night."

"I couldn't afford four packs," Thelma said.

"You don't pay for them," I said and got a look that would peel paint off a wall if there had been a wall with paint. The wallpaper was dark with age and lumpy.

"I'm sorry," I apologized. "I guess I'm jealous of the way

your friends at the bank give you money. I could use a few friends like them."

"That's O.K.," Thelma said, softening up a bit. "They help me out now and then. Good old guys. Most knew my pa before he run off. Old guys ain't my type."

"What is your type?" I wanted to know.

I was afraid she was going to say "Dempsey" when a woman's voice called to her from the next room. "Thelma, who you talking to?"

"Bobby Lee Pomeroy," Thelma answered. She threw her head back and closed her eyes.

"Who in the world is that?"

"Come on." Thelma opened her eyes and motioned to me. "You might as well come and meet Mama."

Mrs. Thompson was in bed all right. Lying there in men's pajamas way too big for her. She was a little bit of a woman with long brown hair that hung past her shoulders. Under a pile of blankets, she was so hidden there was no way of telling if she was deformed or not. Her face was pale to white, and she appeared so delicate, I thought she might break apart if a person talked too loud or shook her hand too hard. I touched her hand carefully, thankful I'd missed stepping on the remains of a cheese sandwich in a saucer on the floor next to her bed.

"Who are you, honey?" Mrs. Thompson asked me in a voice two steps above a whisper.

I told her I was a friend of Thelma's and I had come to give her a paper she needed. I don't know why I whispered, too. It seemed the right thing to do. I liked her right away.

"Now what kind of paper would that be?" she asked, in a normal voice as if I'd passed some kind of test.

The look on Thelma's face told me not to tell, although I didn't see the harm.

"A recipe from a magazine," Thelma said quickly.

"That was mighty sweet of you." Mrs. Thompson nodded. "A friendly thing to do." Her eyes were green like Thelma's. They didn't pierce to make a person nervous like Thelma's do. "I'm glad to know Thelma has a friend. You're the first I've met. She never brings anybody around no matter how many times I tell her it's all right."

"You wouldn't like some of the people I know, Mama," Thelma said. She must have meant the bank guys who were her daddy's old friends.

"Of course I would, child. Why, look at this girl standing here. I like her. You're ashamed of me, that's all. Ashamed of me is what it's all about—" She was ready to say more, but Thelma stopped her. It was a good thing, too, because it was clear she was getting ready to cry.

"Let's not go into that," Thelma said and kind of patted the air around Mrs. Thompson's shoulder. I don't believe she really touched her. "Want tea?"

"No, honey." Mrs. Thompson dabbed at her eyes with the back of her wrist, then suddenly sat straight up with a smile for both of us. "Why don't you two girls have a tea party? Now wouldn't that be nice?" Mrs. Thompson said. You'd have thought we were two little kids. I expected to see a doll's tea set, like you buy in the Five and Dime, come out from under the covers.

"Yes, Mama," Thelma groaned, thinking like me, I guessed, how our ages had been misunderstood. Thelma rolled her eyes toward the door, but I wasn't in a hurry to go yet. I liked being with her mama. I couldn't see why Thelma was so huffy and ashamed to show her off. Honest, I liked Mrs. Thompson the moment I laid eyes on her. Ernest Hemingway would say, "We were *simpatico*." (Did you know he was in the Spanish Civil War? You know who he is, of course.)

"Well, I'm really glad to have met you," I said, with Thelma yanking on my skirt. "I hope to see you again soon."

"Come again, darlin'," she said. "I don't usually have visitors. I expect people have forgotten all about me. Thelma takes good care of me, though. I couldn't ask for a better child. She's my joy."

Thelma had to push me out the bedroom door. I bet dollars to doughnuts her mama could talk a blue streak if you let her, which is something I'd like to do.

"Your mom's nice," I told Thelma. "Does she stay in bed all the time?"

"Except when she has to *go*, if you know what I mean." Thelma nodded in the direction of the outhouse I could see through the window.

"Where's your daddy?" I asked her.

She said, "You tell me."

Thelma and I didn't have tea. She glanced at the essay I'd written and put it on the table. That hurt my feelings because I'd been staying up nights to work on it. I called it: "Hollywood, My Love." That's a nifty title, don't you think?

"You got your picture for the contest?" I asked.

"Not yet. Emory's balking at the price for taking pictures."

"What are you going to do? You can't send in the essay without a picture. The rules say so."

"Well, that's the way things stand," Thelma said like there was nothing she could do about it. "Entering a contest was a dumb idea."

"No, it wasn't," I said, hoping to cheer her up. "Tell Emory how important it is to you. He'll come through, I bet."

We stood there silently looking at each other. Finally, I took the hint.

"I'll see you," I said. "Coming downstreet tomorrow?"

"Maybe," she sighed. I'd never seen Thelma so downhearted. Going back along Pollard, I could feel her watching me until I was out of sight.

Kicking at rocks on the road, I considered the situation of Thelma and her mother. Doc Bowie was right. They're poor as a penny. I feel sorry for Thelma. I don't know how she can get her mother to leave that bed.

Don't you hate it when you want to help somebody and can't think of one thing to do the trick? In a Dr. Kildare movie, I remember a woman who looked some like Mrs. Thompson, lying sick in bed, and Lew Ayres discussing the matter with Lionel Barrymore. Barrymore plays the wise old doctor, ready to help Kildare out of a sticky situation. "She's stubborn," Barrymore was saying inside my head. "You can't help a stubborn woman until she's ready to help herself." The woman was ready, so the movie had a happy ending. Mrs. Thompson is something else!

When I reached the SG, Mr. K. was spreading yards of muslin over the dress pants so the pants wouldn't be soiled during the night with dust and odors—wind or no wind—coming from the Triple H plant.

"You didn't happen to see a redheaded boy go by, did you?" I whispered to Mr. K.

"You got a boyfriend?" he said in a stage voice for deaf people needing their minds read.

"Hush," I said.

But Daddy had heard.

"Boyfriend?" he said, at once demented by the word. "Where have you been?"

I swallowed hard, screwed up courage, and turned up my own volume. "I'm not telling, Daddy," I said. "I'm growing up and I need my privacy."

My speaking up surprised both Daddy and me. His jaw fell. For a moment there I thought mine had, too. I felt pretty good, you know, until Rose spoiled everything by putting in her two cents.

"So—she went to Thelma Thompson's house. Big deal. You know Thelma. The wild girl Emory Jenkins likes."

"What's she doing at her house? With her reputation?" Daddy asked Rose, with me standing right next to him.

"Bobby Lee's helping her get in the movies. It's a contest," Rose explained to Daddy. "You don't have to worry about Bobby Lee. A girl with her nose stuck in a book isn't thinking about the boys."

At that, Daddy said, "Lock up," handing Mr. K. the key, and we climbed into the La Salle. Heading home, we listened to Lowell Thomas on the car radio tell about the GIs fighting at Cassino, a big mountain somewhere in Italy.

It's a tough battle and we don't seem to be doing so well. Daddy shook his head sadly about a dozen times while Rose made *tut-tut* sounds with her tongue.

Living here, the war feels like something happening on another planet. On the streets you never see more than a soldier or two. I don't remember seeing sailors. What you see are guys in work clothes with lunch boxes under their arms. I heard Sid Brammer's mother quit going to church and mixing with people out of pure bitterness because her son is the only one in this town so far to die fighting for his country. When Mr. K. heard, he said sarcastically, "Well, how many would satisfy her?"

Sometimes I think I'll go crazy worrying about Dempsey. I imagine his plane shot down and him parachuting to the ground, then lying in a ditch, watching his whole life flash before him. Driving home tonight, I was afraid my daddy would see my tears in his rearview mirror and say something rude like "What's got into you now?"

I really am crazy about Dempsey, did you know that? I thought you did.

Sincerely your friend,
Bobby Lee

P.S. I'd like to write about poor Mrs. Thompson *and* about poor Mrs. Brammer, too. I would, but I'm waiting on G.A.W.S. to send me those *complete, reliable* instructions. Tell me when they are coming. A postcard will do.

Miss Bobby Lee Pomeroy
Twin Branch, Kentucky
April 29, 1944

Dear Miss Pomeroy:

THE GREAT AMERICAN WRITERS SCHOOL does *not* have an installment plan. However, it has come to my attention that you are serious in your desire to become a writer, and, therefore, enclosed are Lessons #2 and #3.

Lesson #2: *Defining the Short Story* explains how elements of a Short Story are fused by secret techniques we teach aspiring writers like yourself to develop creatively and successfully.

Lesson #3 concerns creating ATMOSPHERE using sensory details for rich and imaginative fiction.

Read the instructions, then write an *opening paragraph* describing a special place to set a MOOD for the story to come. Make the reader SEE the place...a snowcapped mountain, a dense jungle, even a prisoner's cell if you will.

You, the writer, are in Command! It is your job to INTEREST the reader at the BEGINNING. HOLD the reader's ATTENTION! Write no more than 5 SENTENCES. If they are interesting, 5 will do the trick!

We wish to thank you for the dollar ($1) you sent. We hope in the near future you will send the total amount of $10.00 owed to us. (This includes the cost of WRITERS GUIDE.)

By sending these Lessons, we show our faith and commitment to your SUCCESSFUL future. If you wish to pursue a career as a SUCCESSFUL WRITER, you must have no fewer than *all* **10 Writing Lessons.**

Delay no longer! The remaining Lessons remain unavailable until you have completed your financial commitment to us.

Yours truly,
HENRY W. BUCKLEY, PRESIDENT
THE GREAT AMERICAN WRITERS SCHOOL
P.O. BOX 140, KOKOMO, INDIANA

Twin Branch, Ky.

May 5, 1944

Dear Sue,

Lessons #2 and #3 arrived on my birthday! You must have had a serious heart-to-heart talk with your daddy (husband?). I can't imagine what you said, but I sure do appreciate the Lessons. I'm so excited I could spit.

You know, since we've been writing—well, I've done most of it, but it's O.K.—well, since we started this, I feel big changes happening. This morning I asked Annie Sturges to take a look at my hand, hoping this time she could find something. She found the chocolate birthday cake she bakes me every year and she found a pair of ladylike white cotton gloves (her present) that I'll probably never wear.

"I don't see you getting a surprise party, if that's what you had in mind," Annie laughed, "but something special might come in the mail."

That's the first time Annie has been right.

"Now come to Baltimore when I go," I told her. "You can read palms and I can write stories. We'd have a good time." I meant it, too. Annie could pass as white if she wanted. Her skin is about my color and, I swear, *my* hair is kinkier than hers. Annie never takes me seriously. The subject dropped with a thud!

I got to hand it to you people at G.A.W.S. You sure know a lot about story writing. I read *Death of a Traveling Salesman* by Eudora Welty. It's about a traveling man like the salesmen who come through Twin Branch trying to sell my daddy all kinds of sporty clothes for the SG. In this story the salesman's car breaks down on a lonely road and people as poor as the Thompsons help him out.

It's packed with *atmosphere!* I used to think atmosphere meant where the stars and moon were located. I never knew it was an *element* of writing until I read Lesson #3.

I like being 15. I wish I were older, though, and out of here, but I'm not, so I can like it or lump it.

Rose wanted me to have a slumber party like the girls in town do — you know, to have pillow fights, eat fudge, try out hairstyles from the magazines. Some girls might think those things are fun, but I don't. Why do you suppose that is? I know one thing — I don't belong here! I told Rose there was no one for me to invite to a slumber party.

"I've never heard of such a thing!" Rose said, about to explode. "You never listen," I said.

"You must have friends." Rose wasn't listening *still*.

"Well, there's Thelma…," I said to say something to comfort her. "I could invite Thelma. Oh, yeah, and Sylvia Weinstock. She'd probably be hurt if I didn't. The presents would be good." I tried not to burst out laughing. "A prayer book from Sylvia, wrapped in white tissue paper with a red bow. Thelma's would be in a plain brown paper bag. The latest copy of *Astrology Today*."

Rose was not amused. Her face was pink with her irritation with me. "Invite *them*. Invite somebody. It's your birthday!"

"Can't. Just remembered. The Society Club is having its initiation tonight and they are the new members. They have to wear long white gowns and their hair in an upsweep." The outlandish lie made Rose throw up her hands, giving up on the party and maybe giving up on me, too. I scooted out of her presence.

The fact is I hadn't seen Sylvia for a couple of days. I hadn't seen Thelma at Rexall's or at the bank. I hadn't seen Dempsey either. For all I knew, I could have been telling the truth. They *were* busy, but doing what?

Nobody has to guess what I was doing. The usual. Hanging out, against my will, at the good old SG.

"You having a good birthday?" Mr. K. asked me. For my birthday, he gave me a box of handkerchiefs with pink embroidery on the edges from Smith's Linens.

"Dandy," I told him. "Honest. Swell. Real nice." I used my Donald Duck voice.

"It's time you had a change, Bobby Lee, before life passes you by," he said, and, of course, I knew what was coming. "Let me teach you something useful like mind reading. I could teach you in no time. A day, because you're a smart girl. No more time than that."

"How do you know I won't run off with a dog trainer?" I said, which was mean, I knew, but I didn't want to hear about mind reading on my birthday.

"Not you, Bobby Lee. No, my dear, you are a paragon of loyalty," he said, standing tall, with his head at an angle. Ronald Colman again. "I've never known a 15-year-old girl who wasn't chasing boys or disobeying her daddy's wishes. No, child, I'd put my trust in you."

"I'd be more careful if I were you, where I put my trust," I told him, because he doesn't know a thing about me. He doesn't know what goes on inside me. I bet nobody does except you. Would it surprise you if I rode a Blue Ribbon bus to Dempsey's old run-down farm looking for him? I would, too, if I thought I could get there and back without Daddy putting Sheriff Farley on my trail.

I'm sorry about complaining to you this way. Thank Mr. Buckley for my birthday presents. Mostly it's you to thank. I know in my heart if it weren't for *you*, I'd never have the lessons. You're a good person. It's why I forgive you for not writing me. I'd invite *you* to my slumber party if I had one. Would you come?

Seriously indebted,
Bobby Lee

Twin Branch, Ky.

May 10, 1944

Dear Sue,

I was going to wait until I heard from you, but this *couldn't* wait. Didn't I say I should have my head examined for introducing Thelma to Dempsey? I saw the two of them up at the Five and Dime looking into each other's eyes like they were counting the specks.

I saw them, but they didn't see me. I was on Franklin writing my list of sensory details for Lesson #3 when I spotted them. First, I dodged into Fritzie's doorway to keep out of sight. Then, when Thelma turned in my direction, I sneaked into the entranceway of the Bon Ton. I could hear their voices easily and see their reflections in the Five and Dime windows.

"When were you born?" Thelma asked Dempsey. She straightened his shirt collar, which didn't need it. "Tell me the day and the year."

"Well, Miss Curious," he said, "November 9th, 1925."

"You're a Scorpio!" she practically screamed. "I should have known, you wanting to join the Army and all."

"What's that got to do with the price of eggs?" Dempsey said, laughing at her for getting so excited.

"Scorpios are courageous and fearless," Thelma told him in a flirty voice.

"Says who?" Dempsey messed up her hair like she was as cute as Minnie Mouse.

"The stars, you nut," Thelma said, pretending to strike him in the jaw so Dempsey could catch her by the arm.

"You think that stuff is true?" he asked her, putting her arm behind her back, playing, too.

"Well, it's true about you," she said. "Bet they make you a lieutenant before you've been in the Air Force a month."

"I'm aiming for general." Dempsey was serious, of course. Nothing below general interested him.

"You're so adorable," Thelma giggled—a ten-year-old without good sense. "I hear you graduated. Wish I had. I hear the Triple H doesn't care as long as you got eyes to see with and feet to stand on."

"So get a job at the plant," Dempsey said. "It makes things for the war. You'd be helping the war effort same as me." You'd think it was Humphrey Bogart telling Ingrid Bergman to fly out of Casablanca for a good cause.

"If it wasn't for my mama..." Thelma lowered her voice, just above a whisper, to snuggle closer to him. The sunlight had shifted so now they made one giant shadow on the sidewalk. Then there was the swish sound of the glass door of the Five and Dime.

"Work the night shift while she's sleeping," Dempsey said, clear enough. "You could be back home before she woke up."

My heart beat fast as an eggbeater in empty air. To people passing by, I must have looked hypnotized, staring at a headless mannequin in the Bon Ton's window. It was dressed in a red pongee skirt and a blouse to match. I don't know how long I stood there before Mr. Weinstock tapped me on the shoulder.

"You like it? The ensemble?" he asked in a puzzled way. As I said, I was staring.

"Oh, yes, nice," I told him, even though I don't like pongee much.

"Good. Ah, I see you have the tools of your trade," he said, pointing to my notebook and the pencil I had stuck in my hair. "My Sylvia tells me you're a budding writer."

"She told you that?" That shook me up, all right. "I didn't know Sylvia thought I was alive. She never talks to me. She won't even look at me when I talk to her."

Mr. Weinstock nodded his head as if he understood the scene. He's not much taller than I am, so we were pretty much eye to eye.

"She can't help herself," he said, smiling, but sorrowful at the same time. "She keeps to herself too much. I tell her, 'Go out, make friends. Have a little fun. You're only young once. At your age, you're entitled.'"

"You don't suppose she's mad with me for some reason, do you?"

"No, sweetheart, not you."

"The town? Some of the people are O.K., but it's a hick place."

"As everywhere—you find some good people who are accepting, while others ..." He seemed to be searching for the right words.

"Steal your friends!" I blasted out in hope Thelma would hear me.

Mr. Weinstock drew back, startled.

"Sorry," I apologized. "I was thinking about someone—a friend I lost."

He nodded politely. "Well," he said, backing away, "don't let Sylvia discourage you. She needs people to talk to."

"She's got you."

"Fathers don't count."

I was thinking how they did and here I was, standing at opportunity's door, and should knock. "Why…," I began, and it was as far as I came to asking why Sylvia didn't have to work at the Bon Ton. Mr. Weinstock had turned to follow a size 16 in bobby socks inside the store.

Nope! This has not been my day!

When I came back to the SG, I damned Dempsey and Thelma and I picked a fight with my daddy.

"When Andy Hardy wants help, Judge Hardy lends him a helping hand," I said to Daddy, who seemed to be thinking I was something broken he didn't know how to fix. "The judge tells him how to improve himself—how to make his dreams come true. He'd give Andy $10 without Andy having to say a word: 'You need $10? Here, son!'"

I didn't blame my daddy for his confusion. He doesn't like Mickey Rooney much and never goes to Andy Hardy movies, and I was off my rocker!

"I need $10 for writing lessons!" I said, straight out, and took my chances he was willing to listen and be understanding.

"Writing lessons?"

He had been on his way out, but now he was coming back to the cash register where I was standing. He held up his hand and numbered off his fingers. "You were going to be a hotshot songwriter!" went one finger. "A hotshot tap dancer!" another finger. "A hotshot artist!" You have the picture, right? "And now you want to be a hotshot writer?" he said. "Is that what you're talking about?"

"The president of the Great American Writers School said I had fresh, lively talent," I said. (My voice rose in emphasis on the adjectives. I hope you won't give up on me after you read this part, because, you see, I didn't mean to go this far with Daddy. If only I hadn't seen Dempsey and Thelma, none of this would have happened. I don't want you mad at me. I know I shouldn't write about it, but I'm used to telling you the truth. There's nobody else to tell except you.)

"Grow up, Bobby Lee. The man's after money," Daddy said, unusually calm under the circumstances. "Sure, he flatters you and makes you feel good. He says the same thing to everybody who signs up. He sends the same letter to everybody. Next letter says, 'Send money. Send money and I'll make you famous; I'll make you rich.' But no one gets rich except him."

I tried not to cry, but I did. I had worked up to a rain cloud, sobbing into my birthday present from Mr. K. "I could be the best writer in the state of Kentucky. You wouldn't know. You don't care. All you care about is this dumb store. The SG isn't a store," I announced. "It's a *prison*!"

Things went quiet. I could *see* the silence. Thick as brick.

Mr. K. in the front of the store and Rose on the balcony examined both Daddy and me like we were actors in a bad movie and needed someone to write "The End." It was clear neither one of them would get involved.

Daddy was mad, all right. His eyes could have been small, hard rocks. "It may be a prison to you, Bobby Lee, but it was this prison delivered us from hard times. Our good fortune was finding it for sale and having a chance to buy it. It has paid the rent, put food on the table and clothes on your back and mine. Be thankful for this prison."

Daddy loves this store because it did what he said. It brought us through bad times. I was ashamed and truly sorry I'd caused him aggravation.

Seeing Thelma and Dempsey at the Five and Dime is what burned a hole in my heart. I wasn't thinking straight. I'd been thinking Dempsey needed *me* and Thelma needed *me,* and all they needed was each other. At that moment I felt like jumping in the Ohio and would have, too, if it weren't for my Red Cross Lifesaving Badge. Earning it had left a deep impression of the agony of going down for the last time.

I should be writing this to Dorothy Dix for her newspaper column, right? She would publish it, I bet. Well, I chose you. I hope it's O.K. The rest of the day I'm going to feel sorry for myself. I can feel it.

You're not mad at me, are you? If I never wrote you another letter, wouldn't you be sorry?

Your anxious (pen) pal,
Bobby Lee

Twin Branch, Ky.
May 22, 1944

Dear Sue,

I know you think I can't take a hint. I had decided to concentrate on my writing and not think about you *not* dropping me a line and *not* letting me know if you wanted to hear from me. So I've been practicing on my adjectives and adverbs and so far I have 115 sensory details for Lesson #3. Are you interested in reading some? How about: *the gnawing, throbbing pain of a sad and broken heart* and *a soggy, wet pillowcase soaked with searing tears.* Miss Watkins read them and said, "A bit *much*, dear."

Are they?

It's only by accident I'm writing to you. I didn't think I had anything interesting to say until after I'd been out buying Max Factor Makeup of the Stars on sale for Rose and bumped into Thelma's friend, Emory. His old cowboy hat sat low on his forehead. Even then I barely recognized him with his shoulders all hunched up and his hands deep in his pockets. His eyes were blank. I wondered if he'd lost his way to the bank.

"Hi, Emory," I said, calling him by name for the first time.

"Hey, how you doing, kid?" He snapped off his empty sign, and anybody would have thought I was a good friend he hadn't run into for a while. "Grown a couple of inches since I saw you last," he said.

"I've always been tall," I reminded him. Then I couldn't help but ask, "Have you seen Thelma? It's been a month of Sundays since I saw her last." (People talk like that down here.)

"Nobody sees Thelma," Emory said, kicking a cigarette butt off the curb. "Not unless they're working the night shift."

"The night shift?"

"At the Triple H."

"How long has she been at the plant?" I asked because it was news to me. It caught me by surprise.

"Too long. Hell, I have to take my own pants to the cleaners. Do all my damn errands. I reckon it's been a month she's been on the night shift," he said. "And, then, she must sleep all day. If you see her, tell her she owes me some of that money she's making." Anyone could see he was pissed off. They could hear he was, too.

"I'll tell her," I said. "I was on my way over to her place."

I didn't know I *was* on my way over to her place until I said it. Anyway, it was way past time to have it out with Thelma. I tucked Mom's bag of makeup tight under my arm and started that long trek to Pollard Road.

The road was as tacky as ever. The sweet smell from a honeysuckle vine along a fence and the sight of red poppies growing wild livened up the neighborhood some. Several folks had planted Victory Gardens in back of their houses. From the road, I could see beanstalks sway in the fierce wind beginning to blow. Except for scattered dark clouds, it was still a pretty nice day.

Stepping over the broken wooden step to the front porch, I had the beginning of guilt feelings, figuring Thelma might be asleep like Emory said, but then I said to myself, "Well, la-de-da, who cares? I'll wake her if she is."

The screen door wasn't hooked. I went right inside. Red flowered curtains hung from the windows, with creases down the sides showing they were new, but that was the only change I could see since my last visit.

"Thelma," I hollered, "you here?"

A voice said, "Who's that?" and I recognized it belonging to Mrs. Thompson.

"Bobby Lee Pomeroy, Mrs. Thompson," I said. "I came to see Thelma."

"You that little friend of Thelma's?"

"Yes, ma'am."

"Come on in, honey," she said. "Thelma's out, but you come on in and visit."

There she was in bed wearing those old pajamas, propped up against a mess of pillows. Her hair was combed back over her ears and she was wearing makeup—not much. Rouge gave her face a sunny look. Two thin lines of pink traced her lips open in a big smile. A lipstick tube on the windowsill had a greasy rim, but it looked new.

"Where you been?" Mrs. Thompson asked me, as if I came every day and had missed one.

"Working for my daddy," I said. "Where's Thelma? I thought she'd be here."

"Thelma? No, honey, she's taken off somewhere. Don't know where. Buying groceries maybe. That's what she's always saying, 'Be back soon, Mama. Going to the store.'"

I started to ask how Thelma liked working at the Triple H, but the thought occurred to me Mrs. Thompson might not know Thelma was working. Thelma might be sneaking out at night the way Dempsey said she should.

"Did you bring her another recipe?" Mrs. Thompson asked me. "Is that why you came? Well, makes no difference. I'm glad to see you. Glad to have the company. I'm restless today. Must be the warm weather. So, how you been?"

"Fine," I told her. I was standing in the doorway ready to back out, seeing Thelma wasn't around. "You look mighty pretty today."

"Thelma fixed me up," she said. "She likes to play Beauty Parlor. I like it when she does. I get to feeling different, pretending I'm going somewheres important. I am sorry to be in bed every time you come. Ain't no way to greet company, I know." She straightened a faded blanket over her legs like that might help the situation.

"Why *are* you in bed, Mrs. Thompson?" I asked her, surprising myself, the way I blurted it. *Take the chance*, I was thinking. I didn't want to make the same mistake I made with Mr. Weinstock even if it was plain to see Mrs. Thompson wasn't going to get up and go anywhere. "What I mean," I said, as gentle as I could, "is you don't look sick."

She bit her lower lip, thinking the question over. I gave her all the time she needed. "I don't rightly know," she finally said and took a breath as if she was about to tell a long-winded story.

I sat down at the foot of the bed, all ears. The mattress was thin as a slice of bread. I could feel the springs branding my rear end with metal circles. I was uncomfortable, all right, but I meant to hear her out, hoping for a good story to take my mind off a real uncomfortable situation. I nodded my head, showing I was ready and, in fact, in a hurry for her to tell all.

"It was like this," she began in a creaky voice. "Everything bad seemed to come down on me at once. You know what I mean? Well, maybe you do and maybe you don't, you being so young."

"Sure I do." I wanted her to know I'd had experience along those lines. The silhouette of Dempsey and Thelma at the Five and Dime flashed in my mind.

"Sorrow was everywhere I turned like it had wings to follow me. Oh, but it was bad. I was feeling lower than a anthill. I'd been warned. I can't say I wasn't warned. Pluto gave me warning."

"Pluto?" I imagined this big, lovable dog with Mickey Mouse patting his head. "In the cartoons?"

"In the heavens, honey. Like the astrology books say. Don't you follow the stars?"

"No, ma'am. Thelma does," I remembered.

"Thelma buys a new astrology book every month and brings it to me," Mrs. Thompson said. "Thelma's a Leo. That's why she's strong willed."

"What's Pluto have to do with you being in bed?"

"Pluto caught my sign in a bad way. I'm a Cancer. I lost two babies, and my husband run out on me. Like I said, everything bad seemed to come down on me, one thing after the other."

"What was the matter with the babies?" I asked her, not following her line of thought too well.

"Weak hearts, the doctor said. Neither one lasted the week."

Babies dying is a subject that gives me the creeps. I mean I can get chills with goose bumps, trying to understand the fairness of it. You know what I mean? Little babies who never harmed a soul? I got up from the bed then, in a hurry to go. Mrs. Thompson didn't seem to notice I'd moved. I thought she might be in a trance.

"Mrs. Thompson," I said, "you still with me?"

She didn't answer, and I wondered if she went off like that often and if that was her sickness. Then she was talking again. "My, my, so much was happening," she was saying, more to herself than to me. "I couldn't sort it all out, don't you know."

"Someday you will, Mrs. Thompson," I said to finish the conversation, "I'm sure you will." But she was wound up like a Victrola.

"It feels good to talk about those times, bad as they were. Gets it off my chest, so to speak. I married young." She shook her head remembering, looking me straight in the eye. I honestly felt *immobilizated*. There was nothing for me to do except write it all down, because my hands were the only part of my body free to move.

"I was, oh, I guess 13. There I was, a child and married, and quicker than a wink with a baby on the way. Cyril. He died the night he was born, poor little thing. Thelma came after Cyril. She was as healthy as can be. Then along comes Sidney and he died. That boy lived five days and then was gone. I thanked the Lord Thelma was spared. An independent child, she was, too, from the moment she was born, I tell you. Doing for herself and no bigger than a good-size baby doll. I was like that when I was young. *Bigitty*, my ma used to call me. I was smart. A good reader. I loved to read. Thelma didn't take after me in reading. I was heartsick when she quit school. Once when I was just a kid, I found a book on China in someone's trash. After that, all I could talk about was going to China. I'd make plans like I was really going. My ma said, 'Get that crazy idea out of your mind. You ain't going nowheres.' She was right about that. Thelma's daddy drove me to Lexington once. To the hospital they got there for crazy people, you know?"

"What'd they say?" I wanted to know before I made my next move.

"Nothing much. They said I needed rest in bed. Well…" She pulled the blanket up to her chin. "…here I am. In this bed. I haven't sorted out one thing. Do you suppose I ever will?"

"I hope so, Mrs. Thompson," I said, folding my notebook. My hand was tired of writing. Her story wasn't as interesting as I had hoped. *Sorting out things* seemed a puny reason for her lying in bed. I know those doctors in Lexington didn't mean for her to stay in bed the rest of her life. "Don't you want to visit friends? Have a Coke at the drug store? Go to a movie? See about the war in the newsreels? You could still go to China if you put your mind to it," I said. "No one can predict the future."

When I'd finished my speech, I knew I'd done more harm than good. I've seen a kicked dog look happier.

"You're wrong," Mrs. Thompson sort of hissed at me. "The stars can tell the future. They tell you the good and the bad. My stars have never done right by me, though."

By this time the stars had worn me down. "In *Julius Caesar*, William Shakespeare wrote, 'Men at some time are masters of their fates,'" I quoted for her. "'The fault, dear Brutus, is not in our stars, but in ourselves…'" *Or something like that,* I said to myself.

"Well, that's right pretty," she said, cheering up.

"You put too much stock in the stars, Mrs. Thompson. That's my opinion," I said. "I bet you could get out of bed for good if you tried hard enough. I bet you could walk to the end of Pollard Road, if you wanted. Aren't you tired of lying there?" I don't know why I went on like that when I could see she was hurting.

"Sometimes I do get tired, honey," she said, her eyes watering a little. Despite the makeup, her color appeared to be fading. "Sometimes I do get tired of lying here, but it's easier than facing a life bound for nothing, going nowheres."

She turned away from me and left me staring at the back of her head, adding up the years that made her about 35, younger than Rose.

"I'll be going now." My body felt like I'd put a terrible strain on it. I fought a strong urge to crawl in bed next to her for a long nap. "I'll stop by again soon," I said, moving in a kind of slow motion you see at the movies. It wasn't surprising when she didn't answer. From her breathing I'd say she had fallen asleep as I tiptoed out.

The clouds broke open before I reached Franklin Street. Rain fell in buckets, but I didn't run from it. I let myself get soaked. I deserved it. It was my punishment for making Mrs. Thompson feel bad. "Miss Snoop," Thelma calls me. I do snoop. I snoop on Thelma and now her mother and, well, I guess, at one time or another, on everybody in town. But how am I going to learn if I don't Stop, Look, and Listen? Lesson #2 talks about doing that, right?

When I got back to the SG, my clothes clung to me like flypaper. All the Max Factor stuff split the soggy paper bag. I had to crawl under the sewing machine to catch a lipstick rolling under Rose's feet.

"Don't you have sense enough to come in out of the rain? Bobby Lee, honey, you are a sight," Rose said. "What have you been up to?"

I told her the truth. "Playing devil's advocate (*advocatus diaboli*) on Pollard Road," I said, without the Latin.

"Now what's that supposed to mean?" she said, not expecting an answer. "I don't always understand your point."

I didn't bother to explain my point either. My mind was busy calculating ways to get poor Mrs. Thompson to leave her bed without us both having nervous breakdowns and getting carted off to that special hospital in Lexington.

You might be saying to yourself, Why is she butting into Mrs. Thompson's business? The fact is I like her. More than that, I see us as soul mates. If she wants to escape to China, I'll help her pack.

You see how I'm in this thing with Mrs. Thompson up to my elbows. I just need a plan that will work. I'm scouting for ideas, so if you have any, would you let me know? I won't hold my breath, of course, waiting on you. I know better, but...

Always hopeful,
Bobby Lee

P.S. Do you think you could ask your daddy why I owe $10 for 10 *lessons* if the first lesson is *free*? He wrote that April 29, but it's taken this long to sink in. Could you remind him I sent $1 he didn't count? I'd write him myself, but I'm afraid to make him mad. You think you could convince him to send Lesson #4 while you're at it?

B.L.

Dear Sue,

Dempsey is in the uniform of the Army Air Force! Thelma came running into the store saying, "Dempsey's here. Up at the Five and Dime. He's driving his daddy's Buick." I couldn't believe it was Thelma. Her hair was tied with a yellow ribbon and she was wearing a plaid skirt, saddle shoes, bobby socks, and a Peter Pan blouse to match her hair ribbon. Before I even recognized her, she was tugging on my arm, saying, "Come on. He wants to see you."

"What's he want to see me for?" I said.

"He wants to say hello," she said.

She was hurting my arm. "If that's all he wants, tell him I said hello back," I said, trying to shake loose of her. Don't you think she had a lot of nerve popping up like that, grabbing me and expecting me to follow?

Rose leaned over the balcony, dangling a suit coat by the sleeve. "How's the contest going?" she called to Thelma. "You heard anything?"

"No, Mrs. Pomeroy. It's okay. I'm working a job. I don't want to be a movie star anymore," Thelma said.

"You don't?" Rose was disappointed at that. I guess she thought Thelma missed her chance to marry Cary Grant. At times, Rose can be very amusing.

"Come on, Bobby Lee," Thelma said. "He doesn't have all day."

"Rose, you want anything at the Five and Dime?" I stalled for time, wondering if I should swallow my pride, because you know I wanted to see him.

"Emery boards," Rose said.

"We'll get you some," Thelma said, practically dragging me out the front door.

Dempsey was leaning against the fender of the Buick, looking so positively handsome in his uniform I thought I would die right there on the spot. The Army had cut off every bit of his hair, but it didn't matter. He was still cute. I wish I had a picture of him to send to you so you'd know I don't exaggerate.

"Hey, Bobby Lee, how you doing?" He still had that sweet smile. "I thought maybe your daddy had you chained to his store." He grabbed me and gave me a bear hug that sent hot flashes through my body, jolting as electric shocks. "I've missed you, girl," he said. "Didn't have time to say good-bye before I got my call."

"Doesn't he look grand?" Thelma said, batting her green eyes. "Wait till Mama sees him in that uniform."

"Dempsey's going to meet your mama?" I almost added, "In her *bed*?"

"What did you think on D-day, Bobby Lee? Didn't it come off like I told you?" Dempsey said. "Eisenhower was there, calling the shots."

"You run out of pins for your map?" I managed to ask him. I've held my true feelings tight inside for so long, I felt I'd split open like a ripe watermelon if I said more. Besides, my hives were starting up again.

"You remembered about my map, huh? Yeah, I'm almost

out of pins. Say, Bobby Lee, how about you driving to the farm on Sunday?" Dempsey said. "Thelma and I are driving up. I'd like you to come with us. Meet my dad. Ride a horse if you want. You can ride General Eisenhower. He's about your speed."

"I don't know about that," I said. And I didn't!

"You'll come," he said, deciding for me, and off he went to the Rexall to buy Cokes and potato chips to celebrate his being in Twin Branch again.

"You sure have changed, Thelma," I said. "You been shopping at the Bon Ton?"

"Nope. Drove over to Ashland with Dempsey to do my shopping. You like my hair tied up? Dempsey says I look like one of those college girls in the magazines."

"Yep," I said, "Princess Bobbysockser. Never thought I'd see you wearing saddle shoes. Did you buy some Angora sweaters, too?"

"So how you been?" Thelma said, smiling as she changed the subject. "I heard you went to see Mama. That was nice of you, Bobby Lee. Mama likes you a lot."

"I was looking for you," I said. "So was your friend Emory," I added to remind her of the kind of boyfriend she used to have before she got her hooks in Dempsey.

"Oh, Emory," she laughed. "How's that boy doing? I've been so busy I haven't had time to check on what he's been up to."

"Emory told me you're working at the Triple H," I said. "Of course, I wouldn't have known if he hadn't told me. Does your mom know?"

"Sure she does. I'd have told you, too, Bobby Lee, but

I've been awful busy," she said, pouting her lips. I didn't believe a word of it.

"Busy with Dempsey?" I asked her. Right then Dempsey opened the car door, balancing three paper cups in one hand. Thelma's eyes turned soft as cotton when she saw him. It answered my question.

For what seemed like days, the three of us sat in the car, drinking Coke and watching the Saturday crowd. I was alone in the back seat, listening to Thelma badmouth the hillbillies passing by.

"I hear a lot of those guys are being drafted," I said, taking their side against her, you could say. "I hear they make super soldiers and win medals for their bravery." I yearned to be next to Dempsey, but Thelma had opened the back door of the Buick sedan, and gave me a little shove, saying, "Two's company, three's a crowd," pretending it was a joke. Dempsey said, "Aw, Bobby Lee can sit up front with us. There's plenty of room." But I was already in and felt awkward backing out.

I wished I had. I was getting a surge of imagination about the awful things waiting for Dempsey in the air and fighting on the ground while up front Dempsey and Thelma were laughing and cutting up like he was going off on a peaceful vacation. They carried on as if they were King and Queen of the World and nothing could harm them.

"Did either of you read *All Quiet on the Western Front?*" I said in a voice I did not recognize as my own. Dempsey and Thelma both turned to me quick as a finger snap.

"It was written by Erich Maria Remarque," the strange voice announced. "It was a movie, too, directed by

Lewis Milestone with Lew Ayres." I swear, I was switched on automatic.

"I didn't read it." "I didn't either," they admitted in turn, watching me, nonplused.

"It's about war," the voice went on. "The terrible things that happen in war—the ugly, deadly thoughts that travel through a soldier's mind in the darkness of night and him standing in a muddy trench scared he's going to die any minute with a bayonet cutting through his ribs. That's the way it is in a war. Thousands and thousands of soldiers get shot and killed and lose parts of their bodies—see their buddies bombed and blown to bits—" I stopped because I had scared myself and begun to shiver.

Thelma waited to see if I was going to say something more, but seeing me shake, she said, "What's gotten into you, Bobby Lee? You gone crazy?"

Dempsey stretched himself over the back of the front seat to pat me on the knee. "Hey, friend. Don't you worry about me," he said. "I don't want you to worry about me so. I'm going to come back here in one piece. I'm going to come back a hero. You'll see. Why, I'll have enough medals to knock your eye out."

"You don't know what's going to happen," I told him, finding my natural voice again. "No one can predict the future." His hand resting on my knee made me nervous, but it stopped my shaking. I was sorry when he pulled away.

When I read *All Quiet*, I cried the entire day. I thought about Sid Brammer coming home in a box and how he was a young human being who could have been a poet or a doctor or lawyer or anything he wanted because he was smart. Now comes Dempsey, bragging and full of himself, with no more chance in the war than Sid had.

When Dempsey's fingers began to comb through Thelma's long hair, I started to shiver again. Right then, I flipped the door handle and leaped out of the car.

"Daddy'll be looking for me," I said. "I got to go."

"The farm on Sunday. Be ready by 7," Dempsey called after me.

I ran fast, dodging as many people as I bumped into until Mr. K.'s arm stopped me at the door. "Who's chasing you?" he said, searching the street. "There's no bogeyman out there."

I was out of breath and too weak to push him aside.

"You have the heebie-jeebies, kid," he said. "Calm down. I have just the remedy. Mind reading. Let me give you a lesson."

"I don't need a lesson," I said and shook him off me. "I already know how to read what's on a person's mind."

Mr. K. looked puzzled, but he let me pass.

Tuckered out,

B.L.

June 24, 1944
Miss Bobby Lee Pomeroy
Twin Branch, Kentucky

Dear Miss Pomeroy:

You remain in arrears of $9.00. The amount is very small considering the financial BENEFITS that await

you. However, if you think the amount unfair, we are willing to accept $8 if you PROMPTLY send the full amount. We enclosed Lessons #4: *The Art of Dialogue* and #5: *Characterization*, as added encouragement to the development of your writing skills. Don't miss the chance of a lifetime to be a SELLING SUCCESSFUL WRITER! Send money today!

Sincerely yours,
HENRY W. BUCKLEY, PRESIDENT
THE GREAT AMERICAN WRITERS SCHOOL
P.O. BOX 140, KOKOMO, INDIANA

Twin Branch, Ky.
June 30, 1944

Dear Sue,

I'd made up my mind *not* to write to you *ever* again because you *never* write me, but then I received a nice letter from your daddy (?) about the money I owe *and two more Lessons*. It got me thinking that *you* might have come to my rescue again and how much I missed writing to you, so here I am again, letting off steam.

I did drive to Dempsey's farm with him and Thelma. With gasoline rationed, riding in a car only for pleasure and not for work was a real treat. I sat in the back seat again, but I didn't care. If I wanted to be with Dempsey, and you know I did, I would hang on the running board if I had to.

The trip took three hours or so. Dempsey entertained us with stories about horses. He's never read *Black Beauty*. He never saw *National Velvet* either. I told him he should, especially since he liked horses. I was telling him the story of the movie with Thelma interrupting and interrupting, begging us to sing "Don't Sit Under the Apple Tree" and "Row, Row, Row Your Boat." She made such a pest of herself, Dempsey and I agreed to join in. It did help pass the time. Finally, we turned off the highway onto a long winding dirt road. We must have gone a couple of miles when Dempsey said, "Just over the hill."

When we reached the top of the hill, down below was this huge white house, the kind of old-fashioned mansion you see in picture books of the South. I wished you'd been there.

"*Gone with the Wind*," I said. That's what I thought first thing. "Is it Tara?"

"Nope. Fanin Stables," Dempsey said.

"Where are the stables?" Thelma wanted to know.

"About a half mile from here," he said. "I'll show you later."

He drove the car along a gravel driveway past red azaleas and blooming dogwood trees. Here I'd been thinking Dempsey lived in a dumpy old farmhouse with Mail Pouch and Jesus Saves painted on the sides of his barn. Thelma must have been thinking the same, because her jaw hung loose, same as mine.

"There's my dad," Dempsey said. Near the house I could see two colored men arguing with a white man who was dressed in Levi's and wore a cowboy hat like Thelma's friend Emory wears. One of the colored men held the reins to a big, gray, fidgety horse. "It's business as usual," Dempsey said. "The three of them arguing over Bluebell. Russ, the tall one you see there, usually gets his way."

Dempsey left the car in the driveway when a small colored woman, weighing no more than 100 pounds, rushed out the front door and gave Dempsey a smile as tight as a clothespin. "You look like you slept in that uniform. That's no way to entertain young ladies," she said. "Get on upstairs and change."

Dempsey said, "Yes, ma'am," and went running.

The woman was Bertie. She told Thelma and me to sit on the veranda while she made us a cold drink. She made it sound like an order.

"Did you ever?" Thelma whispered to me. "Can you believe this place? Dempsey never let on."

I was glad to hear her say that. At least Thelma wasn't stuck on Dempsey because he was rich. She liked him for himself, the same as me. We were bouncing on those soft, flowered print cushions like a couple of kids when Dempsey's daddy came up the porch steps to shake our hands. He told us right off to call him Clay.

"Dempsey told me about you young ladies from Twin Branch," he said. "I shamed him into bringing you to the farm. You like horses, don't you?" We both said we did, taking our chances with the lie. "Now, who is Bobby Lee and who is Thelma?"

"I'm Thelma," she said, speaking right up, but in a voice as soft as silk and crossing her legs ladylike with her hem over her knees. Ha! Picture it? She wore a blue Angora sweater and white cotton skirt, and, well, fair is fair, she

84

looked pretty. On the other hand, old dumb me wore a green cotton jumper and white T-shirt for the occasion and slouched in my saddles so as not to look 12 feet tall.

"This place is gorgeous, Clay. I've never seen anything like it in my entire life." Thelma was going for the Veronica Lake title. Did you see *The Glass Key*? Well, Thelma did. The silky voice, then tossing her blond hair over her shoulder like the back of her neck was on fire.

"This farm is over a hundred years old. Goes back before the war. The *Civil* War," he said, sizing Thelma up while he was talking. I couldn't tell what he might be thinking. "That war split this state in half, you know. The farm stayed safely on the Yankee side," he said. "But it was touch and go." He went on about the farm, speaking in a low voice so I had to lean forward to hear. Inside my head, I heard Rose say, "Henry Fonda in *Young Mr. Lincoln*." "Older," I said to her, still inside my head. (Do you think I've gone crazy?)

"You're Bobby Lee. Bobby with a 'y'?" Now Clay Fanin gave me the same steady stare he'd been giving Thelma.

"Yes, sir. I am," I answered, but I had to clear my throat twice to get the words out.

"You're going to be a famous writer, I hear," he said, smiling and nodding his head, giving me his personal approval.

Against my strongest will, my cheeks turned hot and surely looked it. "I never told Dempsey that," I said.

"I told him," Thelma piped up like she was my big admirer. "Bobby Lee is always writing. She scribbles secret things in little notebooks, so you be careful what you say around her. She'll write it down for sure."

"Well, if you're going to write about Fanins, you're going to write about horses. We breed them and race them," he said and turned back to Thelma. "This is a man's world here. The only women allowed are Nana and Bertie. They raised Dempsey and take care of me. At night they go home to their own families down the road a piece. Then it's just Dempsey and me having a quiet time, reading and listening to the radio."

Thelma cocked her head like she knew he was making an important point, but she didn't know exactly what. I wasn't sure if he was telling her, "Don't think about moving in" or "If you do, this is what you'd be getting."

Just then Dempsey came back wearing tan trousers and a white shirt open at the neck. I wanted to leap out of the chair and hug him, he looked so good. He took the wicker stool next to Thelma while I tried to hide my disappointment at his not sitting next to me.

"When Dempsey's mama was living," Mr. Fanin said, talking to Thelma still, "she called the farm the loneliest place on earth. 'The end of the earth' she said. She never liked it. It's not a place for women. I've never met one who wanted to stay longer than a cat on a griddle." This time I thought the message was pretty clear: "No women allowed." He turned to me again like he just then remembered his manners. "If you ever want to write a story about horses, let me know. I'm your expert. It's women I never understood." He laughed like this was a big joke, but you knew he wasn't joking. After that, he took off, saying he had chores to do. I suspect he was glad he had an excuse to be rid of us.

Nana brought out a tray of iced tea with fresh mint leaves floating on top of the glasses and a plate of little dainty cucumber sandwiches that only took us a minute to eat. We went to the stables to see the horses and I wasn't a bit scared. Thelma squealed whenever a horse looked at her. Dempsey showed us the horses soon to race at Keeneland and Churchill Downs. He wanted me to ride General Eisenhower, but I said absolutely not. I wasn't going to make a complete fool of myself.

We stayed at the farm until late afternoon. Thelma whined she had to be home early. She's such a fake. She kept tossing her hair over her shoulder like an old towel, and I could see she was nervous. Clay Fanin had followed us for a spell, asking Thelma questions about her family: what her daddy did for a living; what were his *hobbies*. Thelma said her daddy was in the trucking business and gave me a threatening look, turning up the power of her green eyes, so I wouldn't laugh or spill the beans.

Driving back to Twin Branch, Dempsey and I did most of the talking. Horses are interesting, you know. Did you know grass was the natural food for horses? Hay, too. Well, you probably knew about hay. How about calcium and protein? Horses need those. Dempsey knows everything about horses. He says he plans to follow in his daddy's footsteps on the farm. I pray he comes back from the war in one piece.

For the longest time, Thelma chewed on her thumb-nail, saying nothing. She might have been thinking about the farm, it being lonely and no place for women. Clay didn't make it sound very attractive to someone like Thelma who *craves* attention. It wouldn't be so bad for a writer. A writer needs a peaceful place, don't you think?

Dempsey drove me home first. In the morning he'll be on a bus to Cincinnati, then a train to Camp Hood in Texas. "All the way to Texas," I said with my foot firm on the running board, as if that could stop him from going. He crooked his finger at me to come closer so he could give me a peck on the cheek. A "so-long kiss" he called it, not "good-bye." I grinned. *Grin and bear it*, I told myself. "See you soon, Dempsey," I said. I didn't want to think about him going and me maybe not ever seeing him again. That didn't come to mind until I was left alone at the curb watching the car's red taillights disappear around the corner.

I sat down on our porch steps. The street was as quiet as the inside of a coffin. A full moon was up and I stared at it for the longest time, not wanting to go in, but not wanting to stay out there either. I hoped Dempsey's car would come back down the street, but of course it wasn't about to. He and Thelma would be headed for Pollard Road or they might park first on Heavenly Hill, where couples go to kiss and wish on falling stars.

Sitting on the steps all alone put me in mind of a poem Edna St. Vincent Millay wrote. Part of it goes:

> *Love has gone and left me, and the neighbors knock*
>   *and borrow,*
> *And life goes on forever like the gnawing of a mouse.*
> *And to-morrow and to-morrow and to-morrow and*
>   *to-morrow*
> *There's this little street and this little house.*

My thoughts turned to Dempsey's mother. I wondered what she looked like. Does Dempsey have her red hair? Where did she live before she married Dempsey's daddy? Did she love him? How did she die? Was it of loneliness? Can a person die of loneliness? Sometimes I think it could happen. Do you know?

Rose startled me, turning on the porch light. "You're missing Edgar Bergen and Charlie McCarthy," she said. "Judy Garland's going to sing. Come on in now."

I came inside and upstairs here to my bedroom. I got in bed with my clothes on, too tired to put on pajamas. Even though I closed the door tight, I can hear the radio. Judy Garland is singing, "Get Happy!"—making it sound easy as pie.

Your "Melancholy Baby,"
Bobby Lee

Twin Branch, Ky.
July 17, 1944

Dear Sue,

You know how I've felt about Sylvia Weinstock, right? She's totally ignored me. Left me talking to myself. Well, today I decided the time had come to tell her what a pill she was. How rude she was, too. By now you know as well as I do where to find her, and there she was in her booth, reading, and, of course, ignoring me standing beside her. I raised my voice, causing Doc to look out from his office, and recited, "'The time has come,' the Walrus said, 'To talk of many things: Of shoes—and ships—and sealing wax—Of cabbages—and kings.'" And, hey, a miracle happened! Sylvia put down her book and she said, "'And why the sea is boiling hot—And whether pigs have wings.'"

Talk about shock. My hair could have stood on end!

"Lewis Carroll," she said.

"Charles Lutwidge Dodgson," I said. "Lewis Carroll was his pen name. His *nom de plume*. That's French."

"*Oui*," Sylvia said and actually grinned.

I swear to you this is all true.

"'The Walrus and the Carpenter' is my favorite," Sylvia said.

"I can recite it from memory," I said, taking a chance she wouldn't ask me to do it. "Look, I'm sorry if I interrupted your praying."

"Praying? What praying?" Obviously, Sylvia didn't know what I was talking about. "Why would I be praying?"

"Isn't that what you do?" I said.

"Not here. Not in a *drug store*," she said.

"I've seen you," I told her. "In this very booth. You've been doing it for weeks."

"Oh." She nodded. "I see what you're saying. No, I'm not praying. I'm studying for my confirmation."

That was a relief. I don't mind her being a loner, but I'd be put off by an out-and-out weird person.

"What church do you go to?"

"I don't go to a church. I'm Jewish," she said as an explanation of sorts. "I'm going to be confirmed at the Agudath Achin Temple in Ashland."

"A *temple*?" I said. I knew nothing about a temple in the town of Ashland, which is a good distance from Twin Branch—which is not strange because the Weinstocks are the first Jewish family I ever knew personally. "I don't get it," I said.

"It's a Reform temple. Ashland is the nearest town with enough Jewish people to support a temple, a place where Jews can worship and carry on traditions."

So there we were—talking. Frankly, I didn't care what we talked about. It didn't matter. Mr. Weinstock would have been proud if he had seen us, which he didn't. Don't get me wrong—we never got chummy to the point of talking about boys and a sleepover, but, hey, Sylvia acted like a civilized human being. I sat down across from her. Standing next to each other, we'd make a Mutt and Jeff couple.

So, O.K.—Sylvia is a loner who keeps her thoughts to herself. I do, too, except when I'm writing to you. Remember Rowena in *Ivanhoe*? She had beautiful dark eyes and pale skin you'd die for. That's Sylvia. (Rowena did have pale skin, didn't she?) Rose had pegged Sylvia as Elizabeth Taylor in *National Velvet*. Maybe. One thing for sure— Sylvia and I are the only girls in Twin Branch who don't wear makeup. Oh, wow, you should see the girls at our school, shoveling on makeup in the girls' room and wiping it off with paper towels before going home to their church-loving mamas. Get me out of this town! Please!

Seeing Sylvia had finished her drink, I asked, "How about a cherry smash? My treat." I was at the soda fountain like a shot before she could refuse. "Don't go away," I said, but I could see that she wouldn't. I thought, *She likes me. What took her so long?*

I carried the glasses back to the booth and we talked about this and that. I asked if she liked living in Twin Branch. "Not much," she said, and I told her I didn't either.

"Don't you hate the hillbillies who come into your store? Their *mentality*?" I think now, that was a snobby thing to say.

"I admire the hill people," Sylvia said like she was putting me in my place. "I think they must have a hard life. It's very cold in the winter. Farming the rest of the year couldn't be easy either. It's admirable the way they survive and create music and care for nature."

What she said was a bit highfalutin, but it did call to mind *The Trail of the Lonesome Pine* with another Sylvia (Sidney) living in the hills like an admirable person, and I promised myself to be less of a crab when Saturday rolled around. I asked her about Miss Watkins.

"I like her," she said. I was glad to hear she did. "She can be a drill sergeant on punctuation," Sylvia said. "Especially the use of the comma." I added my vote to that.

"Miss Watkins supplies me with books from her own personal library," I said. "I'm reading *Wuthering Heights* by Emily Brontë." I didn't mention why. I didn't mention you either.

"She must think you're very smart," Sylvia said.

"I'm not. Sid Brammer was smart. People say he was the smartest student the school's ever had."

"Did Miss Watkins give him books?"

I don't know. I wonder if she did. "I didn't know Sid well, but I was very sorry when he was killed."

"People are being killed in the war every day, every hour, every minute," she said softly. "This very moment while we're talking and drinking sodas, people are being killed somewhere. Soldiers on the battlefield. Old people sitting in their homes. Children who never hurt anybody in their lives." Sylvia's eyes had filled with tears. A strange, uneasy feeling I can't describe began to creep over me. "Whole families disappear from the face of the earth just like that," Sylvia said and snapped her fingers. "There's a sudden knock at the door. The sound of machine-gun fire. Then silence and death."

I hadn't bargained for the change in our conversation. One minute we're playing Alice Through the Looking Glass and the next Looking Through the Valley of Death. It was scary. Sylvia reminded me of somebody, but I didn't know who at the time and I couldn't figure out why I was shivering.

Sylvia had bowed her head, and with one finger she traced the outline of a heart someone had carved into the wood of the table. She had gone back inside herself.

I counted to 10 before I interrupted whatever she was thinking. I couldn't resist the question. "Why don't you help out in your daddy's store?"

She raised her head and blinked. I expected her to ask who I was and what I was doing in her booth. "You mean work?" she finally asked. "Why I don't work in the Bon Ton?"

"Yes, work. Help out. Take cash. Make boxes. Wait on customers. All that," I said, making it as clear as I could.

"My father won't let me," she said.

I waited for more. Nothing. "You mean you actually

asked him and he said no?" I wanted to make sure I had this straight. "Why? Is it against your religion?"

Sylvia studied me — I supposed, to see if I was serious. "It's not against our religion," she said, blinking again. (She needs to have her eyes checked.) "Why would you think that? We have hired help."

"My daddy has hired help, too. Mr. K. But *I* have to help out." Sylvia shrugged. "You're a lucky duck, is all I can say," I told her.

I said the trigger word, not knowing it at the time, but she jumped right on it. "Yes, you're right! I'm lucky. Damn lucky," she said. "I'm lucky to have my parents. Lucky to live where I do. Lucky to be alive. I have all the luck. Dumb luck is what life is all about, isn't it?"

"Well, I don't know if I'd go that far," I said. Her eyes were filled with tears again and I felt it was my fault. It was like she *was* Elizabeth Taylor, but her horse had lost the Grand National. I didn't have a clue to what brought on the explosion. The good time had disappeared. "Do you believe in the prophecy of the stars?" I said to say *something*. "I've got a friend who does. She believes the stars predict a person's luck, good and bad."

"I have to go," Sylvia said. When she stood up, I saw she was wearing the red pongee I'd seen in the Bon Ton's window. It looked nice on her.

"I wish you didn't have to go," I declared. "How about tomorrow? Same time? Same station? You're not going away for the summer, are you? Do you go to camp? I don't. Will you be here?" I was still asking questions after she ran out the door.

94

When I got to the SG I said to my daddy, who hadn't said anything to me, "It's not because they are Jewish. Sylvia Weinstock's daddy says she doesn't have to work because he has hired help."

"So?" said Daddy, unimpressed by the news.

"Why is *she* the lucky duck? What about me?"

Mr. K. put in his two cents. "Remember that old saying: 'The grass looks greener on the other side.'"

I easily ignored him. "Mr. Weinstock said he'd give Sylvia $10—$20, anytime, just like that." I snapped my fingers. "No questions asked."

"So?" Daddy said again. We were standing face to face, waiting to see who would turn away first. It was me. I mean I. It was *I*! Of course! That's the way it always is.

To write you this, I'm balancing the stationery on the narrow ledge of the balcony and my stupid pencil keeps slipping off. Meanwhile, Rose is humming to herself while operating on a pair of brown twill pants. A pile of pants waits for her on the sewing machine. Rose is complaining in whispers, but I can hear her.

Lesson #4: *The Art of Dialogue*—I think I like this one best so far. How about having two girls in love with the same boy meet at the train station? They are strangers and it is *hate* at first sight. The boy is a soldier and both girls are waiting to wave as his troop train passes. The train comes through, but he is not on it. Now they don't hate each other. They talk (dialogue) and become friends. So you like it?

Earlier I wrote how Sylvia reminded me of somebody, but I couldn't recall who? Michele Morgan in *Joan of Paris*! Did you see it? Paul Henreid was a pilot caught behind Nazi enemy lines and Michele was the passionate Frenchwoman who risked her own life to save his. The movie got four stars ★★★★!

I have one more question. Be honest now. Do you really think there is an *art* to writing dialogue? Sounds pretty fancy for what my daddy calls "chewing the rag." Art or chewing, I'm glad Sylvia is doing it with me. Wish you would.

Yours in friendship,
Bobby Lee

July 26, 1944
Bobby Lee Pomeroy
Twin Branch, Kentucky

Dear Miss Pomeroy:

We at THE GREAT AMERICAN WRITERS SCHOOL understand a student's occasional interest in the lives of the professional staff employed here and the desire to exchange opinions on world and personal matters. However, COMPANY POLICY prohibits the exchange of letters between staff members and school students.

CONSIDERATION for our students' SUCCESS initiated this policy allowing students to think only of writing their very BEST without distraction or concern for and by staff members.

We see no need for a further explanation.

Sincerely yours,
HENRY W. BUCKLEY, PRESIDENT
THE GREAT AMERICAN WRITERS SCHOOL
P.O. BOX 140, KOKOMO, INDIANA

Twin Branch, Ky.
August 15, 1944

Dear Sue,

In case you don't know, your daddy (?) wrote me a letter about company policy and now I understand why you haven't written to me. It's a big relief to know the truth. You've probably been dying to answer my letters, but didn't because it was against the rules, right? Well, I hate to put you back into the frying pan, and I wouldn't if it weren't for Clay Fanin. I need advice. This afternoon, he was here in Twin Branch in *person*. You surprised? So was I!

At first, I didn't recognize him sitting next to Doc Bowie at the counter having coffee and he didn't recognize me. We hadn't seen each other since I visited the farm. When I saw it was Dempsey's daddy, I should have scooted out. *Trouble*, I said to myself, but it was too late. He was all smiles, knowing who I was. He shook my hand like an old buddy and bought me a Coke. I knew we'd better get straight to the point of his visit, so I asked what he was doing in Twin Branch.

"Oh, passing through is all," he said.

"That's the best way. Pass *through*," I said. There was no way to believe he was telling the truth.

"This is a nice little town," he said, taking in the view of Franklin through Doc's dirty windows. "I like it."

"You'd change your tune if you lived here. I like Baltimore," I said, "where we lived before coming here."

"Oh, sure, Pimlico Racetrack," he said. "That's all I know

about Baltimore. Have you been to the track?"

"Not that I remember," I said.

Then we talked about Baltimore, with neither one of us knowing very much about the city. We struggled to make conversation, which, I suppose, is why I confessed my plans for the future, and he bent his head to listen as if he cared about my life, and I knew he didn't.

"Do your mother and daddy know you're planning a trip?" he asked on his third cup of coffee, adding enough milk and sugar to make a baby happy.

"We haven't had a serious discussion, if that's what you mean."

He straightened his shoulders and gave me a stern fatherly look any kid would recognize as a starter for a lecture. "You ought to be thinking about college," he said. Now, that surprised me. Men usually say, "Find a husband and get married"—not my daddy, of course. Mr. Fanin said, "You ought to get yourself a good education while you're young."

"Miss Watkins, my English teacher, tells me the same thing, but my daddy has a different idea. He wants to keep me a slave in his store," I told him, overdoing it a bit. "Daddy won't let me go anywhere."

He picked up our check and slid off the counter stool. "Your daddy doesn't want to lose his little girl, that's all. You can't blame a father for loving and wanting to hold on to his child."

He put his arm around my shoulders to add to his understanding of how deeply my daddy feels about me, but it didn't surprise me when, in his next breath, he asked about Thelma. I knew that's what he'd come for.

Had I seen Thelma? Where? What was she up to? Who with?

Well, I hadn't seen Thelma for a while and had no reason to look for her. When I had seen her, she was with those guys at the bank. I didn't tell him that.

"She might be working the night shift at the Triple H."

He raised his eyebrows. "I didn't know she worked at the plant," he said. "Doing what?"

"Beats me. Ask Dempsey, why don't you?" I recognized it as a stupid thing to say *after* I said it. Dempsey, more than likely, didn't confide in his daddy any more than I did in mine.

Then Mr. Fanin put me in a terrible spot. He asked me for directions to Thelma's house. I didn't want to tell. I didn't know if he wanted to cause trouble or what. But I didn't want to lie either.

"It's a good ways," I dilly-dallied. "A long ways from here. Hard to get to. Awful hard."

He said, "I have my car."

My mind snapped a pitiful picture of his big, shiny Buick stuck in a ditch on Pollard Road and a bunch of ragged kids raiding it for parts. My imagination was running at full force and there stood Thelma in a tacky housedress and bare feet answering our pounding on the front door. The visions were fuzzy, like you see in a horror movie, but Mrs. Thompson was napping, plain enough, in those old men's pajamas.

"Come on with me," Mr. Fanin said, as I feared in my heart he would. "You wouldn't want me to get lost, would you now?"

99

"Aw, nobody gets lost in Twin Branch," I said as he took my arm. "Look, I'm only on a Coke break." I tried to explain. "My daddy gets violent when I'm gone too long."

"We won't be long."

I knew there was no use. Clay Fanin is a man who's used to getting his way.

The Buick was parked in front of Fritzie's. Fritzie waved to me and I waved back, hoping he'd come and save me from the trip. He didn't. Mr. Fanin motioned for me to sit up front with him when this time I actually preferred the back seat. *If this causes trouble, Dempsey won't ever forgive me,* I told myself. *Thelma will kill!*

Today, luckily, Pollard Road was bone dry and no apparent danger to cars. Mr. Fanin, taking no chances, drove slow enough to pick flowers. I watched his face while he inspected the junky cars, the porches piled with trash, and kids running wild in the yards. He studied the scene like he was preparing a report for President Roosevelt on the conditions of poor people. By the time we reached the end of the road, he was pale as vanilla pudding.

"This is it," I said, pointing to the Thompson house. "Thelma lives here."

"Here?" he said, but it sounded more like "*Not* here!"

He stopped the car, keeping the motor running. I didn't need to look again to know he was a man in shock. What did he expect? The Taj Mahal? My daddy taught me being poor is no crime, but Mr. Fanin looked ready to make an arrest. Dempsey must take after his mother.

We sat quiet, me not looking in his direction for love or money. Five minutes must have passed, maybe ten! Then as calm as you please, he backed the car all the way up Pollard Road — backed it, mind you — and drove me straight to the SG like wild animals were chasing us. I expected to see Sheriff Farley hot on our trail. It's like people say: when you want the sheriff, where is he?

Mr. Fanin double-parked in front of the SG with the motor going. "Thank you, Bobby Lee, for your time," he said, wearily.

"Thelma has an awfully nice mama," I said. It was the only thing I could think to say and mean it. "You'd have liked her if you'd gone inside and met her."

"What got into my boy, do you suppose?" he said. "Did I do wrong raising him without a mother? Is it the war?"

"I think you were probably a good daddy," I said. What else could I say, right?

"I see young men sign up for the war," he went on, not paying any attention to me. "I see them marrying girls they wouldn't have looked at twice in peacetime. Marrying and shipping out. When they come back — it'll be divorce time. That's what's going to happen. Hundreds, *thousands* of couples, with babies, standing before a judge saying they'd made a big mistake and want out, and Dempsey could be right up there with the rest of them."

The steam seemed to have gone out of him. He'd lost the bright-eyed, bushy-tailed look he'd had earlier. For a moment there, I felt sorry for the man, but, call it a *second wind* or whatever you want, in the wag of a dog's tail Mr. Fanin was back to his old bossy self. "Remember, missy, what I told you. Go to college. You get yourself an education even if you are a girl. No matter," he said. "Girls can learn, too."

The car door was barely closed before the car zipped ahead, leaving little clouds of Pollard Road dust hanging in the air. I had no time to kick his fender, which was something I felt like doing. Girls can learn, *too*? What kind of remark is that? Doesn't he know about Mrs. Roosevelt? Madame Marie Curie? Harriet Beecher Stowe???!!!

Look—I really appreciate your reading this. Who'd have thought Clay Fanin could get me fired up? I hope I don't get you in trouble with your daddy (?) for writing you again. You tell him I said this is a free country and that's what our men *and* women are fighting for. His company policy is un-American and probably unconstitutional! People should be able to write to anybody they want to write to. I don't care if he's your daddy or husband or the iceman, his policy is unfair.

You agree, don't you?

Yours for independence,
B.L.

Twin Branch, Ky.
August 29, 1944

Dear Sue,

Guess what? The Zachem Circus is in town. Thelma had something *special* to tell me, and that is why she stopped by the SG today to invite me to go to the circus with her. Daddy said O.K., just like that!

"You been drinking 'the milk of human kindness'?" I joked.

Daddy snapped right back with "You know I don't drink milk." So much for quotes from the *Shakespeare Reader* Miss Watkins loaned me.

The circus is set up in that field on Pollard next to Thelma's house. The town sent men to clean up the trash and garbage to make room for a big tent and smaller ones for sideshows, causing a big to-do in town. For 10 cents a body could park in front of a dumpy house of his choice. If a car owner doesn't pay, he might find a headlight missing or his tires flat.

Zachem has never been to Twin Branch. No circus has that anyone can remember. The Triple H, paying for 3 shifts of workers, might have been the big attraction for the circus to come now. There's plenty of money begging to be spent.

Zachem is a middle-sized circus with Mike Zachem both owner and lion tamer. Thelma and I had been on the circus grounds for only a short time before we met Mike himself. We were standing outside the main tent buying cotton candy when he came strutting by in his white knickers and pith helmet and started up a conversation with Thelma. He stared deep into Thelma's eyes like he'd lost something there. I think the guy with him was a kind of bodyguard because Mike Zachem is a celebrity and not bad to look at, even up close. Mr. Bodyguard was the one with a fresh mouth.

"Well, aren't you the little passionflower," he said, looking Thelma up and down. "You transplanted here or is this your natural habitat?"

Thelma gave him a blank stare. I don't think "habitat" is in her vocabulary. "You girls like the circus?" Mike Z. asked.

"Never been to one," Thelma piped up, biting into the fluffy pink lump we'd just bought. "Aren't you scared to get in a cage with lions and tigers? I'd be scared as all get-out."

"No," Mike said, pretty modest about it. "I've been doing it a long time."

Mr. Bodyguard said, "He could teach you how it's done if you want to learn."

Ole Mike smiled, letting Mr. B. do the talking. Thelma chewed on her lip like she was actually thinking it over. She started tossing her hair — you know, the old Veronica Lake routine — and blinking those two green signals of hers. Mr. B. began questioning where she lived and all that, like he would deliver Mike Z. right to her front doorstep if she wanted.

I thought she was going to give him the information, but she didn't. "Far from here," she said, and the guy not knowing he could have thrown a rock and probably hit her house.

Thelma backed away from the two of them, saying she and her girlfriend (me) had to run. We had an urgent appointment on the other side of town. Mr. B. gave her behind a pat and we walked off. Fast!

"Aren't they something else?" Thelma said.

"Mike Zachem's in the movies," I said.

"So?" she said. "Who cares?"

I thought she did!

"Now, Bobby Lee, what would I do with either one of those old men? You want a lion tamer? Then you tell him where *you* live."

"He didn't ask me," I said. I did sort of wish he had. I would never have told him. I'd like the experience of saying "No."

Thelma was pumping me up with peanuts and more cotton candy for what, I hoped, was not going to be a dumb favor to spoil the afternoon. The weird people in the sideshow had already unsettled me some, and after Thelma paid our admission to the Big Tent, a bunch of crazy clowns surrounded us, taking us "prisoners" to our seats. You'd think they'd been waiting for our entrance. Well, for Thelma's. One clown gave me a balloon with Zachem's face for free because I was with her. Jeez!

At the high point of the show, when Zachem entered the big cage of lions and tigers, Thelma tugged my sleeve. "Let's go," she said.

"Now? Why now?" I protested.

"Mama might be hungry."

"Can't we get her and bring her back?" I said. I thought it was a bright idea, you know, just the ticket to lure her out of bed.

"Mama says she can see all the circus she wants from her bedroom window."

"I could try," I said. "We can both give it a try."

"It's no use." Thelma was on her feet. "Anyway, I want to talk to you about something important. Let's go."

Kicking at anything in my way, I followed her. I'd looked

forward to Zachem snapping his whip and lions making sounds you don't ordinarily hear in Twin Branch. That's why I came in the first place. "So now what?" I said sarcastically once we were outside. "Another movie contest?"

"No, that's in the past."

"So?" That girl can get on your nerves. The longer she kept me in suspense, the madder I got.

As we snaked through the refreshment stands, Thelma offered to buy me a hot dog, which I refused, and showed an unusual concern for my safety when a horse appeared to eye us suspiciously from a makeshift stable.

"Get to the point," I said.

Finally, she did — almost. "I invited you today because I promised Dempsey I would. Dempsey told me to make it my business to get you out of your daddy's store. Dempsey said you needed to have some fun."

"What else?" I said. I knew there was something else. With Thelma, there had to be.

"O.K.," she said. "I want you to write to Dempsey."

"I do," I said. "Are you kidding? I write Dempsey even when I don't hear from him."

"I mean for *me*. Write for *me!* Look," she said in that rough old voice I hate, "I can't be bothered writing that boy letters every day like he wants. I can't think of anything to say. There's the weather and, yes, I miss him. Oh, it's *boring*. I want you to write interesting letters for me. You pretend to be me. Get it? I'll pay you for each letter you write. How about it?"

"You'd pay cash?" *Cash* is the magic word, you know.

"Please, Bobby Lee, say you will. Think how happy

you'd be making Dempsey. He's lonesome down there in Texas and needing some loving words."

"Dempsey knows my handwriting," I said, but also thinking here was a chance to be out of debt to you-all.

"I have a friend at the plant who can type. She said she'd type any letter I wanted. I'll tell Dempsey I'm learning to type and I'm practicing on him. A letter a day. A dollar a week—no, I'll make it $1 and 50 cents. How about it?"

"What should I write?" I said, knowing I was caught.

"Write him anything you want. I don't care," she said, "as long as he gets a letter every day saying I'll be here waiting for him when he gets out of the Air Force."

You probably think I should have my head examined. Lowell Thomas says GIs are desperate—that was his word—*desperate* for letters from home. I'd be doing a patriotic act, right? Well, right or wrong, Thelma and I shook hands on it.

After we left the circus grounds, we walked to town in the hot sun. I left her in front of the bank with Emory and the others. Soon as she squeezed in, Emory had his arm around her like he owned her. And she *let* him! I was tempted to back out of our agreement on the spot. I would have, too, if I hadn't been in front of Rexall's window and over bottles of Jergens Lotion I could see Sylvia on the other side. She was a pitiful picture. Sorrowful. I thought she was crying.

I went inside and handed her the balloon the clown had given me. Unfortunately, Mike Zachem's face had shrunk and his grin disappeared. It's the thought that counts, isn't it?

CONTINUED—

Last night I was too tired to finish this. I hit the bed like a sack of bones. It's early A.M. Rose is in the bathroom putting on her Max Factor. Daddy's downstairs eating prunes, 3-minute soft-boiled eggs, toast, and coffee. His breakfast is always the same. Annie's giving him her personal weather report straight from the arthritis in her left leg.

I'm writing this in bed. If I'm late for school, I'll say Mom didn't wake me in time. Everyone does.

Picking up from yesterday—you'd have thought the balloon I gave Sylvia was explosive. "What am I to do with this?" she said, sniffling and shifting the string from one hand to the other.

"It's supposed to cheer you up." My throat was dry from the dusty walk and hot sun and I wasn't feeling swell myself. My blouse stuck to my back with perspiration thick as paste.

"My father wants to take me to the circus," Sylvia said, pinching Zachem's shrunken face. "He knows what I'm going to say. I don't want to go. It won't stop him."

"Want to trade daddies for a while?" I said. "My daddy never invites me anywhere—except the SG, of course."

Sylvia managed the straight-pin smile I'm used to seeing. When she lifted her face, I watched a couple of left-over tears roll down her cheeks. "I want to join the Army," she said.

"Hey, join the *Navy*!" I said, like the Navy recruiter does on the radio, trying to humor her, you know. "'Join the Navy and see the world!' You want to see the world, don't you?"

"I want a gun," she said, softly. "I want to fight. I want to kill people."

"Did you read *All Quiet on the Western Front*?" I asked her.

"Yes," she said. "Why?"

"Just wondered," I said, seeing how I couldn't give her the speech I'd made to Dempsey and Thelma. I hadn't expected her to say yes. You know in the comics when somebody gets an idea a balloon pops over their heads? Well, right then, one exploded over mine.

"Sylvia," I whispered, though no one was near us, "you have family in Germany? In Europe?"

She nodded. "In Paris," she said.

I could have kicked myself. I've been so slow seeing her problem.

"We think the family is there," she told me. "My father sends money to the old address, but we don't know if they receive it or not. There's no way to know for sure."

"Gee, Sylvia, I'm really sorry." I meant that with all my heart. "Why are they there and you here?"

Sylvia told me her Uncle Philip wanted to stay in France where the Weinstock family has lived for generations and her daddy wanted to seek his fortune in America. Her uncle has or *had* an antique store, a family business.

"I have many cousins, but Lore is my age. I'm closest to Lore," Sylvia said. "We've been writing to each other since we were little kids. It has been months since I had a letter from her. We haven't heard from any of the family."

"Don't they have friends you could write to and find out about them?"

"We've tried. Nothing. We hear from no one. I dreamed about Lore last night," Sylvia said. "Two men were taking her somewhere. They were rough with her and she was crying and trying to pull loose."

"That was only a dream," I said, trying, you know, to ease her mind. Sylvia had twisted all the straws from the straw holder into tight little wads of paper. Doc will have a fit when he sees them. "Your cousin could be in hiding. The whole family could be hiding in a barn or in a cave — some place like that."

I was actually describing a movie I'd recently seen at the "X."

"No, the Nazis are everywhere. People tell on one another. They'd be caught if they tried to escape. I think they have been caught already." She rubbed her tears, leaving streaks on her cheeks. "I want to *do* something, but there's nothing I can do."

"I know what you mean," I said.

"No, you don't!" she said. Then she did it to me again — she jumped up from the booth and deserted me. I was actually shaking, I was so angry with her for doing that.

"Damn her!" I said, because I *did* know what she meant.

Sylvia had left in such a hurry, she forgot her prayer book. I stopped by the Bon Ton to return it, but the front door was locked. I figured her daddy had closed early to take her to the circus after all, so I brought the book home.

I'd never seen a Jewish prayer book. Half of the words were in English and half in Hebrew. I didn't know what the wiggly lines were until Daddy told me it was the Hebrew. He knew, he said, because when he was a kid, he lived on Lombard Street in Baltimore. "There were Jewish refugees there, right off the boat," he said.

"You mean, *before* Hitler?"

"Jews have been refugees for a long time," Daddy said. "You can find Jews in every country in the world. You've heard about the Wandering Jew?"

"It's a vine."

"It's a Jew without a country. The ones admitted to the States were the lucky ones."

"How do you know so much about Jews?" I was curious, but, also, this was our first discussion on something serious.

"You think you're the only one who ever read a book?" Daddy said and turned his back without waiting for an answer.

Funny that Daddy used "lucky" the way Sylvia did — except not as sarcastic.

Luck is a mysterious thing, don't you know. Some people have good luck and some people have bad luck. Why? Do you think it has something to do with God? I'm going to ask you this — if I learned to pray and was religious, what kind of luck do you suppose I'd have? Harriet Beecher Stowe was a very religious person who had good luck. Her *Uncle Tom's Cabin* was published and that made her famous. Miss Watkins said it wasn't HBS's writing, "it was the *times*," but wasn't she lucky to be writing at that time?

Here it is *time* for *school*. Oh, well...Keep in touch!

Your inquisitive friend,
B.L.

P.S. You might want to tell your daddy (?) now that Thelma is paying me for letters, I can pay him for my lessons. Tell him *his* luck is about to change.

Twin Branch, Ky.
September 11, 1944

Dear Sue,

After complaining about no mail, *two* letters came today!
I loved the one from Dempsey with a snapshot of him in
front of a tent, aiming a rifle at his buddy taking the picture.
Dempsey writes that Texas is flat as a pancake. He says he
fiercely misses the Kentucky hills, Bertie's sweet-potato
pie, and the Rexall Drug Store. Of course, he misses Thelma!
Thelma's letters, he says, have become *soooo* interesting and
funny. He reads them again and again. That made me feel
like an awful fake! A big *jealous* fake!

Now, the second letter is going to surprise you. It's from
the *Editors* of the *Saturday Evening Post*. How about that?
They write: "Thank you for letting us see your manuscript.
We appreciate having the opportunity to read and consider
your work and are sorry we are unable to use it. THE
EDITORS."

I pinned it to the bedroom wall—my first letter from
an Editor. *Nota Bene* (Latin): they said they are "sorry" they
couldn't publish it. Aren't you proud I finally sent a story
into the wild blue yonder? I found the address in your
superduper *Writers Guide*.

Would you like to see the story I sent? About Mr. K.?
It's about how he teaches a girl (guess who) his mind-
reading act and how they travel around the world meeting
all kinds of interesting people. They get rich and split
because he is kind of a jerk and she meets a really good
joe and falls for him. Well, like the *Guide* says, "Try and

try again," so *Liberty* magazine gets the story next. Keep your fingers crossed.

I stuck the letters in my pocket when I went to see how Mrs. Thompson was doing. With Thelma on night shift, I figured Mrs. T. might be lonely and like some company. I needed some myself. The letters had me pretty excited. Feeling my oats, so to speak, I showed Mrs. T. the letter from the *Editors*, and when she asked if she could read my story, I pulled it right out of the envelope and handed it to her.

While she read, I made tea. There was a box of graham crackers on the shelf, and when I brought it all on a cookie tin as a tray, she raised her hand to silence me as she finished the last page. "Bobby Lee," she said, admiringly, "this is the *best* story I ever read in my life. I never knew mind reading could be so thrilling. The way that Mr. Hemingway could get up on a stage and help people with their lives, well, it touched my heart."

"His name is Mr. Kleykamp. I changed it to Hemingway," I said. "I was writing about Mr. K. He works in my daddy's store."

Mrs. T. has taken to wearing mascara—Thelma's doings—and her eyes seemed unnaturally large and ready to pop out with surprise. "You mean you were writing about a *real* person? Someone you know?"

"Yes, ma'am," I said, glad to see my story made such a hit. "He's real, all right. Some of the story is even true."

"That's a man I'd like to meet," she said, her head nodding in quick moves you see chickens make, pecking feed. "I truly would like to meet that man."

"Are you serious?" I asked. She kind of startled me, being so lively all of a sudden.

"Why, yes, I am. Is he still heartbroken over that no-good Roxy?"

"Shirley," I said. "Shirley is her real name." I wrote about Mr. Hemingway's partner running off before the girl joins the act, but I didn't mention she was his wife. "Look," I said, leveling with her, "Mr. K. isn't as good-looking in real life as I make out in the story. In fact, his hair is going gray, and for all I know his teeth may be false. He talks a blue streak and tells the same stories over and over until you want to climb the wall. He tells one about entertaining President Hoover that most likely isn't even true."

"Lordy, he's done some traveling, hasn't he?" Mrs. Thompson said, ignoring the facts I had given her. "Been everywhere. Do you suppose he's been to China?"

"He never mentioned China. Not yet. Look," I said, catching her fever, "if you're sure you want to meet him, I might be able to arrange it." When I said that, she sat straight up in bed and started combing her hair. "I'll ask," I told her, because I was thinking a woman who combs her hair sudden like that might also be ready to put on clothes and get on with her life. "I can't promise he'll come here," I warned her.

"Of course you can't, honey," she said, not very convincingly. "I know that."

"He might not want to come all the way out here to Pollard. How about meeting in the park? How about Rexall's Drug Store?"

"You're a right sweet child. I know you'll try," she said, which I took to mean she wasn't about to leave the bed yet. Well, a promise is a promise. That's how I left it.

I didn't show Mrs. Thompson my letter from Dempsey—too afraid my feelings toward him would show through. I kept it warming my pocket. The only person who sees Dempsey's letters is Annie Sturges. Her nephew is stationed in Texas, too. He's in a separate Negro unit, which is crazy when you think on it, because it's the *same* Army fighting the *same* enemies. Her nephew's letters mostly complain about treatment from the white people living near his camp.

"I don't need him to tell me stories about crackers," Annie says. "I still live in this world."

Annie prefers Dempsey's account of Army life because he describes every little thing soldiers do from morning to night. Annie says the both of us know enough about basic training to sign up for combat ourselves.

You might like to know I'm having a good time writing my "Thelma letters" every day. I like thinking up funny stories about what happened at the Triple H—and it didn't, of course. Charlie Chaplin helped me once. You know that movie called *Modern Times*? Remember when Charlie is working in the factory and can't keep up with the assembly line and the machines attack him? I had Thelma say something like that happened at the Triple H. Not serious, you know. I hope Dempsey laughed. Thelma never said. She never does.

One thing—the Thelma letters are never romantic. If Thelma wants that stuff, she can add it herself. I'm not writing it for any amount of money.

Do you know the writer Willa Cather? Did you ever meet her or read her books? In *O Pioneers*, she writes (for this character who is she) that she likes trees because "they seem more resigned to the way they have to live than other things do." I found that peculiar. What's so good about being *resigned* to the way you have to live? Nothing I can think of. I can't imagine being *resigned* to living in Twin Branch. I don't plan to be *resigned* to anything—except, maybe, to love.

Omnia vincit amor (right?)
B.L.

Twin Branch, Ky.
September 17, 1944

Dear Sue,

The weather is crazy. It's September and hot as a furnace, which is why I'm here at Mayo's Beach on a Sunday with my parents. Mayo is what they call a *beach* in these parts. What it *is* is a stretch of *mud* along the Big Sandy River. *Mud* is not beach, but hillbillies don't know the difference. Wow! A cool breeze has finally come down the mountains.

My daddy is watching the old woman who sells sodas and sausages from the back of her Dodge pickup. He's funny the way he shakes his head and moans, "What I wouldn't give for a bucket of crabs." He says the same thing every time he sees her and repeats a long tale about eating 2 bushels one afternoon on the Maryland shore. Daddy misses Baltimore, same as me, but he's not griping.

Annie packed us a basket of fried chicken, potato salad, coleslaw, and biscuits, and we are waiting for someone to give up a picnic table in the shade. I'm in charge of getting the table. My eye is set on one, which means I might have to stop writing and hop to it at any second.

Don't have much to write about. Nothing much has happened. I'm down in the dumps, but that's not news. I need somebody to talk to, so you're elected. See, I didn't want to come here in the first place! I'd rather be home listening to records. Daddy said my face was so long I'd *step* on it unless someone was around to warn me.

HOLD IT!

Well, I got a picnic table, but I had to fight a hillbilly to do it. He jumped out of the bushes like a grasshopper. "Beat ya!" he said with a Bugs Bunny grin on his face. "No contest."

"Not so fast," I said. "I touched it first." I had my pinkie on the wood.

"Beat ya fair and square," he said and began slapping the tabletop, thinking he was Gene Krupa on drums. "Over here!" he yelled, and his family came running at the same time Daddy arrived with our food.

"Is this our table?" Daddy asked, looking from me to the hillbillies.

"I would have sworn it was," I said.

The woman put a gallon-size Thermos on the table and, sizing up the situation, said, "If it's just you-all and us'ns, there's plenty of room."

"And my wife," Daddy said.

"Of course, your wife," she said like she knew he had one.

They introduced themselves as the Burt family. Mrs. Burt wore a sunbonnet from the Five and Dime and Mr. Burt was wearing—you guessed it—his best Big Ben overalls. *Dumb as tree stumps*, I thought, just as Daddy said.

"I want a swim," the hillbilly guy, whose name was Charley, began whining like a little kid. But let me tell you, old drummer Charley is big enough to pass for a man any day. He could model for those ads showing a big bully with muscles kicking sand in some poor little guy's face. Charles Atlas Bodybuilding—that's it.

Well, Charley is *not* the guy in the sand, by a long shot. He started for his swim toward the river, walking backwards with that silly grin on his face and all the while giving me a wicked eye.

"I'd swear that boy was a fish if I didn't know better. Charley'd stay in the water all day, all week, if we'd let him. Call me Pearl Mae," Mrs. Burt said to Rose. "This here is my husband, Crawford, and sister here is Lilylu." Lilylu was a skinny little thing I guessed to be about 5 years old.

"I've never heard the name Lilylu," Rose piped up like she was a name expert.

"Well, it's really Lucy Lily, Lily being a family name, but somehow it got twisted and so it's Lilylu now."

"That's cute," Mom said. Whether she meant it or not, it opened a boring conversation about people's names.

"I'll eat later," I said. I put this letter aside and carried my book down to the riverbank. It was poems of Edna St. Vincent Millay. You know how "Renascence" starts out with

"All I could see from where I stood"? Well, when I settled down all *I* could see from where I stood was Charley Burt. I tried to keep my mind on the poems, but I couldn't. That Charley Burt turned out to be the best swimmer I've ever laid my eyes on. Forget about Johnny Weissmuller and *Tarzan*. Charley could outstroke Weissmuller any day in the week. I hated to admire him, but I did. When he got out of the water, he flopped down beside me.

"You ever go in?" he said, panting for breath. "Or are you one of those pretty girls who comes to show off her bathing suit?"

"I swim," I said, pretending his freshness didn't bother me. "The Red Cross taught me."

"Nobody had to teach me," he laughed. "Papa just threw me in the river. It was sink or swim so I swum."

"What a way to learn," I said. "Primitive, really."

Then Charley began to ask me personal questions like he was a private investigator—where did I live, the name of the street, did I have a steady beau, what was his name? Then he wanted to know why I'd bring a book to the beach. What was I reading?

"Do you know anything about poetry?" I said, pretty rude. "Have you ever *heard* of poetry?"

"I know a poet," he said.

"You?" I fairly snapped at him. "Who would you know?"

"Jesse Stuart," he said, and I felt the flush rising on my face. Miss Watkins thinks Jesse Stuart is the best writer in the state of Kentucky. "He lives near our place," Charley said. "Sometimes I stop by with Mama's root beer. She makes good root beer."

"What do you talk about?" Meaning, of course, what could he—Mr. Hillbilly—talk about with Jesse Stuart. I was being rude long after it was time to quit.

"Nothing special," he said. "I tell him about Daisy, my dog. Smartest hunting dog in these parts." He rolled over on his back and stared straight into the sun without blinking. "We don't talk about poetry, that's for sure. I don't know nothing about poetry."

"You ready to join the Army?" I asked him.

"Get myself killed? Heck, no. What did Uncle Sam ever do for me?" He had a high-pitched laugh I didn't like much. "I'm 16. I'm too young to die."

As it turned out, Charley's family was from Boone Mountain, but I was wrong about Charley. He isn't dumb. He can play the guitar and read music. Lucky for him the teacher could teach music and every other subject you can name in the one-room schoolhouse at the bottom of Boone.

"Do you learn much?" I asked.

"Don't want to learn much," Charley said. "I can read and I can write and that's more than my daddy can do."

It turned out the Burts don't own a radio. He knows about the war from his teacher, but during school vacations he falls behind on events. The Burts disapprove of picture shows, dancing, whiskey, and a lot of other things. They belong to the Church of Christian Messengers for Redemption by the Holy Spirit. If I hadn't written it quickly, I'd never have remembered it.

When we got back to the table, our moms were talking about this and that and Daddy was telling Crawford Burt about the Cincinnati Reds and how much money he'd lost betting on them. Gambling was another thing the Burts were against, but Mr. Burt listened politely. That's one thing you can credit to hillbillies. They can be very polite in conversation.

Charley and I had a piece of chicken and an apple before Charley crooked his finger at me, telling me to follow him up a path to a spot overlooking the river. We sat on a flat rock he called his "throne" and had a first-rate view of the sun setting behind the hills in fiery red colors. That's when Charley took my hand and held it the way Annie does when she's tracing the lines, but I knew he wasn't thinking about finding my future.

I don't know why I let him kiss me. I hadn't been kissed since I played Spin the Bottle in the 6th grade. Charley's kiss was a lot like a Spin the Bottle kiss—his dry lips pressed against my dry lips. I closed my eyes and tried to pretend he was Dempsey, but my heart made it plain he was only a boy taking up Dempsey's space.

Charley whispered, "You are a wonderful girl, Bobby Lee."

It puzzles me how he came to that conclusion after a couple of dry kisses. If those kisses were supposed to lead to that *one thing* my daddy talks about, it would be slow going. The fact is I was starting to feel blue again, wishing I had someone close by I could care about. Before the tears broke the dam, I excused myself and went back down the path.

When we were ready to leave, Charley asked for my address and telephone number. I wrote both on the brown paper bag he handed me.

On the way home Rose said, "Didn't Lilylu remind you of somebody?"

Neither Daddy nor I were interested enough to answer. That didn't stop Rose. "Remember *Little Miss Marker?* Remember Shirley Temple in *Little Miss Marker?*" she asked, turning to Daddy. "Didn't she remind you of Shirley Temple?"

Daddy speeded up, still saying nothing, but shaking his head at the poor quality of the conversation. Daddy will never understand o-b-s-e-s-s-i-o-n if he lives to be a hundred. Rose waited for one of us to answer, so I said, "Yes, she does," but it wasn't true. Lilylu was no more like Shirley Temple than Charley was like Dempsey.

To tell the truth—I wouldn't mind if Charley wrote. Thelma must get lots of sweet letters from Dempsey that I never see. Why can't somebody write me a sweet letter. I say: Write! Somebody! Anybody! Even a hillbilly will do!

Your frantic friend,
B.L.

P.S. The dollar bill I Scotch-taped here goes to your daddy (?) toward he-knows-what. Thanks.

Twin Branch, Ky.
September 24, 1944

Dear Sue,

Did I tell you I hate Sundays? This morning the telephone rang and Rose called up to me, "It's a man for you, Bobby

Lee." My spirits started to rise up, thinking I don't care who—even Charley—you remember the guy at Mayo's Beach? It wasn't. It was Clay Fanin wanting to know if I'd seen Dempsey. I told him I hadn't laid eyes on Dempsey since he left for Texas. The mail situation wasn't good either.

"Russ swears he saw him in Twin Branch on Saturday wearing a cowboy hat," Mr. Fanin said. "He was with your friend, Thelma, going into a movie theater. You telling the truth?"

"Yes, sir," I said. "As far as I know it."

Dempsey's daddy is demented, you know that? I don't like Thelma being Dempsey's sweetheart any better than he does, but it's not fair to spy on them. I did once and I'm sorry I did. Russ probably saw Emory with Thelma—which is not an easy mistake to make, with or without a cowboy hat, but Russ might have been in a hurry. Since it was Saturday, he might have been *drunk*!

This being Sunday, and me bored out of my mind, I figured the time had come to keep my promise to Mrs. Thompson. I went over to the boarding house where Mr. K. stays and found him in a granny rocker on the front porch, dressed up in a seersucker suit, cool as a bucket of ice. We talked about the weather and how there was nothing to do in Twin Branch on a Sunday except go to church and neither of us had a mind to do that. I waited for the right moment in this boring conversation before I made my announcement. "You have a secret admirer," I said. Boy, that caught his attention like a crash of thunder.

"Who be it?" He'd stopped rocking. "Give me the scoop," he said.

"A pretty woman," I said. "Only thing is she's mostly confined to her bed."

"A cripple?" he said, frowning at the news.

"No, sir," I told him. "She can walk as good as you and me. She needs cheering up, is all. I've told her about you and she would like to meet you. She could use the company."

"So could I," Mr. K. said. "I never liked putting my anchor in a small town."

"Me neither," I said.

"I need to get back in show business."

"The way things are going, I might go with you," I said. I wasn't serious, though.

"People here are too damn God-fearing for their own good." He stood up, ready to move now. "You say this woman is a friend of yours?"

"One of my *best* friends," I said, smiling.

"Is she a churchgoer?"

"No. You can bet on it," I said.

"Well, in that case," he said, "lead me to her."

I congratulated myself. Here was the chance to make good on my promise to Mrs. Thompson and at the same time check out Mr. Fanin's suspicion, which had me curious.

Walking along Pollard Road, Mr. K. had the same sour look as Clay Fanin. Kids were running wild to the music of an old Maytag washer, causing him to move faster. "Are you sure you know the way?" he asked, irritated and probably sorry he'd agreed to come.

"Don't you worry." I tried sounding cheerful. "I've been here hundreds of times. I know my way, all right."

Right then a fat kid driving a homemade go-cart of milk cartons deliberately tried to run him down. I pushed him out of the way, but I give him credit for not turning back right there and then. I would have.

At the end of the road, I said, "This is it, Mr. K. You know what people say, 'Don't judge a book by its cover.' Wait here till I call you."

I found Mrs. Thompson asleep. I shook her by the shoulders, saying, "Where is your brush? You got a comb? Any makeup? You got a visitor." When I told her who it was, she started straightening her covers and moaning, "Oh, no. Oh, no. Why didn't you give me a warning? He can't see me like this." I peeked out the window, fearing Mr. K. had run off, but he was waiting while Mrs. Thompson fixed her hair and painted her lips with a lipstick I found on Thelma's bureau. She changed from her pajamas into a new pink cotton gown I'd dug out of a drawer. So Thelma wasn't keeping all the money for herself. I stuck my finger with one of the straight pins I pulled out and sucked the blood to stop the bleeding.

I didn't care about a little blood because that woman was picture perfect. When I brought Mr. K. in, she was as pretty as any movie star you named. Mr. K. pulled at his tie when I introduced them, and then he puffed up like a rooster. I carried in a chair from the front room and left them alone to get acquainted.

In the kitchen I put water to boil in the kettle for tea, and then, I'm not ashamed to say, I snooped in Thelma's room. Snapshots of Dempsey in his Air Force uniform were stuck in the sides of the mirror on top of the bureau. In the closet I found skirts and jackets on hangers, never worn, with the price tags still on them. Ten pairs of new shoes—I counted them—were lined up along the wall.

The closet was neat, but, oh, her room. The bed hadn't been made in a month. She must have a dozen pillows, all crumpled on one side of the bed. I was thinking what a good detective I'd make, picking up blond hairs and observing only one impression on the sheet. Happily, I never found a sign of Dempsey.

I could hear Mr. K. turning on the charm. Out of habit, I had the image of him as Fred MacMurray—MacMurray in the bedroom with Mrs. Thompson, played by Barbara Stanwyck. They played together in *Double Indemnity*, where they plotted to murder Stanwyck's husband. Luckily, Mr. K. and Mrs. T. won't have a problem since Mrs. Thompson's husband has already flown the coop.

I served them tea on a wooden board I used for a tray as if I were the Thompson maid. I took a magazine to the swing on the front porch, *obviously*, keeping out of their way while waiting for the visit to end. All there was to read were those old movie magazines Rose had given Thelma, so I read how Hollywood was snubbing Lew Ayres because he was a conscientious objector. If I'd known this would be a long visit, I'd have brought a book to read. *Gone with the Wind. Anthony Adverse.* Something big! Inside Mrs. Thompson was laughing like a couple of circus clowns had dropped by. What could Mr. K. have been saying?

It was late afternoon when I decided to break up the party. I didn't care a fig if Mr. K. did give me a nasty look for interrupting his act. Seeing I wasn't going to budge from the doorway, he got to his feet.

"It was a pleasure conversing with you, Adeline," he said, calling her by a name I never knew was hers. He bent over the bed to kiss the back of her hand. Her cheeks were flushed like she ran a temperature. And that was it. The visit was over.

Back on the road, Mr. K. was all smiles. He wasn't bothered one bit by the smell of cabbage cooking or the Sunday preaching coming from half a dozen radios. By the time we reached paved street, he was whistling and patting his hair. The tune sounded like "Sweet Adeline." When I asked if it was, he shrugged, but he didn't fool me. I don't have to be a mind reader to know he was thinking about one pretty good-looking lady.

A person feels good after doing a good deed. I figured I'd done two in one day—counting my check on Thelma's room. If Mr. Fanin calls again, I can relieve his mind. Dempsey was not on Pollard Road. The news will surely make Mr. Fanin happy. It does me!

Your good scout,
B.L.

Twin Branch, Ky.
October 8, 1944

Dear Sue,

Yesterday was Sylvia's confirmation in Ashland. I drove there with the Weinstocks in their Oldsmobile and we got to talking about books and you know what? When I told them the books I'd been reading, they knew every one of the writers—Hart Crane and Willa Cather and William Faulkner (Miss Watkins's favorite) and the others. I don't mean they knew them personally. They had read their books. Amazing, right? Well, I started to stutter and I've never stuttered before, but I was excited having this kind of conversation with Sylvia's parents. It's the kind of conversation I wish I could have with my own parents, but, well, Daddy says he reads books, only I see magazines. Rose likes the magazines, only mostly about movie stars—so there you are. Mr. Weinstock likes Hemingway same as me, but he doesn't like him shooting animals. Mr. Weinstock is a vegetarian. I told him I was considering it. Actually I'm not, but I wanted to say something to impress him. Mr. Weinstock calls his wife a "Mozart freak." "She only likes biographies of Wolfgang Amadeus Mozart," he said in a full voice like an opera singer. Isn't calling her a "Mozart freak" a comical thing to say?

"Not true." Mrs. Weinstock punched him lightly on the shoulder. "I play him. I don't read him." She turned around to me to explain she plays the piano. I figured as much.

God! Sylvia is a lucky duck. I bet dollars to doughnuts she doesn't know it.

"My mother is a 'movie freak,'" I said. Don't ask me why I said it. I was glad no one did.

The temple is nothing like a church. No steeple, no bell, no cross to be seen, and all that. This one was on a side street where people lived in houses and there were no stores. Kids played Go Sheepie Go in an empty lot and some big boys were tossing a football when we drove up and parked.

The temple is built of white stucco and has two white marble pillars, one on each side of the entrance at the top of some cement stairs. The roof is a white dome. It reminded me of a wedding cake without the bride and groom — a big piece of white confectionery sugar in the middle of the block.

The Weinstocks and I had front-row red cushioned seats that were connected to each other, the way they are at the "X." Looking around, I counted about 100 people. Women wore hats and carried gloves and were nicely dressed. So was I. Rose bought me a frilly dress from the Bon Ton I'll never wear again, pink cotton with little bows down the front so I look like Deanna Durbin in *One Hundred Men and a Girl* — except I'm taller and I can't sing.

Sylvia's dress was the prettiest. It was white silk with long sleeves. Her mother persuaded her to go to Mildred's Beauty Parlor for a pageboy bob — the latest thing. Sylvia tried fluffing it up with a brush before we got out of the car, but Mildred had used a wave set and it was stiff as cardboard. Sylvia and I both hate fashion. We have that in common.

Besides Sylvia, there was a small mousy girl and a guy with a bad case of acne being confirmed. The preacher — *rabbi* — said the three of them were "the hope of the future." Sylvia groaned when she heard that. Rabbi Daniel Gold was a student rabbi from the Hebrew Union College in Cincinnati. It's called H.U.C. The congregation is too small to have a permanent rabbi. He looked young, all right, and uncomfortable on the platform. He was short and on the skinny side—I was thinking a leaf could knock him over until I heard him speak. He said, "Open your prayer books to page 20." What he lacked in weight he put in his voice, and the seats vibrated! Later, he told me himself that H.U.C. believes strongly in voice training and projection. He must have an "A" in the course.

The first two speeches were O.K.—a lot of thanks given to mothers and fathers and teachers, and much was said about "why we go to Sunday school." Sylvia's speech was the last, and if I'd been her, I'd have been chewing my shoelaces. Not her. Sylvia was Joan of Arc going into battle. She took long, sure strides toward the lectern and quick hops up the three steps to the platform.

"When the first American GIs entered Paris, I was listening to the news on the radio," she began. "I was listening at home, by myself, when it was announced that American soldiers had, at last, reached Paris, France. I listened to the descriptions of the joyful welcome of the French people who crowded along the road as the soldiers marched by. People were crying and waving French flags and throwing flowers and throwing kisses, and, just as if I were there, with them, I began to cry and wave my pretend flag. I imagined the brave American soldiers coming through our front door and parading in our living room, past the couch, past the piano, toward the stairs, up the stairs, filing through every room of our house…I was *thrilled*," she said, and with that, she pulled me out of my body so I kind of floated above her. I almost stopped breathing. She made me see what she saw. She drew strong pictures of her happiness for all of us sitting there to see. She wanted us to share her excitement, and, I swear to you, people did. I did. It was in the air, you know, so we felt a great shock when Sylvia shouted, "Heil Hitler!"

The room was eerily silent until Sylvia said, "While we celebrate, thousands of people continue to suffer under the rule of Hitler and the Nazis. We can't forget them." Sylvia, then, told the congregation about her relatives in France, pretty much the way she had told it to me. "My Uncle Philip and his family are there. They may not be alive."

Her face was wet with perspiration. Under her arms two damp spots widened on the white silk and I began to sweat because she was sweating.

She told us that her family heard stories of what actually happens in the work camps—the *slave* camps. The stories tell of prisoners starving and tortured and how they disappear hundreds at a time. The camps, they say, are really *death* camps, too horrible to imagine, where Jews are sent because they are Jews.

"I've prayed for God to stop the suffering, but I don't believe He listened," she said. "I've begun to believe He doesn't care. If He did, *you* tell *me* why He allowed this terrible injustice to happen."

Well, no one told her. We all shifted around in our seats. A few people coughed or sighed. I felt tired—drained, you know. Sylvia asked us to stand and together pray, "one last time to change God's heart."

I bowed my head with the others. I don't know how to pray so I didn't say anything. I was relieved when Sylvia asked us to sing the Marseillaise, but, then, I don't know that either.

Everyone applauded Sylvia for her swell speech. I was proud to be her friend, if that's what I am. After Rabbi Daniel Gold said a closing prayer, people crowded around Sylvia to congratulate her. Some shook her hand. Some hugged her. I hugged her, too. She gave us all her tight little straight-pin smile.

A small, gray-haired woman smiled at Sylvia sweetly, saying, "There will always be questions we can't answer, dear." Sylvia gave her an icy "Why?" that sent shivers down my back.

The celebration party was one flight down in the basement. Folding tables were set with trays of food—a huge fish with an open belly of soft, white meat, herring in sour cream, orange slices of lox (I was told) on black bread. "You never had a blintze?" a woman said to me. "You haven't lived."

A turntable played recorded music and people danced something that wasn't exactly a square dance, but about as near as it can get. Billy (the kid with the acne) asked me to dance. The dance was easy to learn. Of course, I was 12 feet taller than he, but he was a good dancer and awfully nice. Everyone I met was nice. I met a woman who said she used to live in Baltimore, too. She knew *Liberty Road!* If going to Dempsey's farm was the best day of my life, this turned out to be the second best.

"How can a person be Jewish?" I asked Sylvia.

Sylvia nibbled a piece of honey cake. I could see she wasn't especially interested in explaining. "You are born Jewish or you convert," she said.

"How does a person convert?"

Sylvia shook her head. "Forget it, Bobby Lee," she said.

"Why should I?" I said.

"Because it's not for you. Anyhow, it's dangerous." I made a face, showing that was no answer. "Do you think only Nazis hate Jews?" she said, not waiting for an answer. "There are people right here in Twin Branch who hate Jews. My mother is afraid to answer the phone. I have to answer it. People say nasty things and hang up on me. We get letters in the mail saying we deserve to suffer and *die*."

"Are you saying you'd be better off if you weren't Jewish?" I asked.

"No, *you'd* be," she said, "not me. I'm glad. I know who I am."

I envied Sylvia Weinstock, who knew who she was. I wished I could say I knew who *I* was. I mean *deep* down inside. You know what I mean? How I *fit* in the world. If I were Jewish, at least I'd know that much.

We didn't say more about it. Sylvia did one of her famous get-up-and-leave-Bobby Lee stunts, so I danced with about everybody and Mr. Weinstock practically had to drag me out.

It was late when they dropped me off. Back home Rose wanted to know how the confirmation went. "I'm thinking of becoming Jewish," I told her.

"That's nice," Rose said, half listening as she switched the dial, searching for some radio show, I didn't know what.

"Did you hear me?" I said. "I think being Jewish will help me with my life."

Sometimes I think Rose should have her hearing checked. In my heart I know Rose loves me, but I need her to *listen* to me, too.

"It's the *Jack Benny Show*," Rose said, ending the search. "Alice Faye is a guest. She's married to that bandleader on the show. Oh, what's his name?"

"Harry James." I get irritated and give her wrong answers on purpose. "I'm converting to Judaism," I tried again. "Tomorrow."

"Phil Harris," Rose corrected me, as if I didn't know. "Alice Faye is married to Phil Harris."

"Right," I said, hopelessly. "How about me running off to China to work with Baptist missionaries?"

"Harry James is married to Betty Grable," Rose informed me. "So how did you like the confirmation?" she asked.

Sometimes I think I was adopted. How else could Rose be my mother?

I bet you're thinking the same as I'm thinking: it's time to move on with my life, and if that means getting religion then I guess that's what I have to do. You wouldn't know the names of Jewish writers I could read, would you? I'd ask Miss Watkins, but I don't want her in my business any more than she is now, which is too much. If I converted to Judaism, do you know if I'd have to learn Hebrew?

Pax vobiscum,
Bobby Lee

P.S. The dollar ($1) goes to your daddy. Tell him I said, "Hi." Well, considering company policy, you'd better not.

Twin Branch, Ky.
October 26, 1944

Dear Sue,

You remember Charley Burt? The hillbilly at Mayo's Beach? Well, he drives to Twin Branch in his dad's pickup pretty regularly now. You know what else? My daddy likes him. I'll go so far as to say Daddy *loves* him! Doesn't that blow your mind? It's because of the way Charley makes it his business to help out in the SG. He pitches right in when we are busy and he's a good salesman. Mr. K. says Charley's taken to the SG like a duck to water, and here's something else—old Charley doesn't give me the time of day when he's helping out. Do I care? No, I don't. I'm glad he likes working at the SG.

In fact, Charley's arrived at the right time, because Daddy can't count on Mr. K., whose mind is definitely not on his work. Customers practically shake him to get his attention. He daydreams worse than I do. He leans on the showcase with his head in his hand and stares at the fluorescent lights above his head. I tell him he'll go blind if he keeps it up. Last week he bought a pair of ladies' shoes at Fritzie's. Black pumps with high heels. I know the shoes weren't for his landlady. Does that give you a hint about where his mind has wandered?

I heard my daddy tell him, "The best thing for you is a *legal* divorce." My ears stood up like they'd been dipped in starch.

"I can't get a divorce," Mr. K. said. "The wife has disappeared. Vanished into thin air. Coburn, who used to book us, says he hasn't laid eyes on her or that damn fool she ran off with. He thinks they left the country. Went up to Canada. He doesn't know for sure."

"Bigamy is a serious offense," Daddy said, but I'd think Mr. K., being a grown man, could figure that out for himself.

Daddy and Mr. K. were sitting side by side on the wrapping table. No customers were around. I'd never known them to have a personal chat. Rose and I watched them from the balcony, trying to hear what was going on.

"I think you should divorce your wife. Do the right thing," Daddy said. "Go up to Lexington and hire a detective to find her."

"Sam Spade," I called down to them. "Dick Tracy."

"Not the right time for jokes," Rose told me.

"Those private eyes take you to the cleaners," Mr. K. said as if he'd had personal experience. "I'll give it some thought. I'm in a bit of a jam. My lady-friend is in a hurry to hear wedding bells. She's in a hurry to get on the road, too. She's talking about *China*."

When he said that, you can bet I was straight out the front door on my way to the Thompson house.

The minute I pushed open the screen, I sensed something was different. Then I saw Mrs. Thompson sitting in a chair reading one of those old movie magazines, looking sweet as candy, dressed in a red and white striped housedress. A thin red ribbon caught her hair in a ponytail. I swear on a Bible, she was better looking than Thelma!

"Why, look who's here!" she said with a big smile. "Where in the world have you been?"

"You're up," I said foolishly. "Out of bed." I noticed the black pumps she was wearing right away. "What happened?"

"Astro-Carto-Graphy," she said. "It changed my life."

"Oh," I said. "I thought it had something to do with Mr. K."

"Well, Tippy helped, too," she said.

"Mr. Kleykamp? *James P.* Kleykamp?" I asked her, needing to know for sure.

"Tippy is his stage name," she said, which was news to me. "Isn't it cute?"

Then I got a full explanation about how her life changed when Mr. K. gave her the money for an Astro-Carto-Graphy map. The map showed her how she had been misreading the stars for years and how she had been missing out on the good things in life.

"I've been so *wrong,*" she said, wide-eyed. "My misery had long passed. Good fortune was waiting for me to notice. You see, Venus was standing in my path. I hadn't seen her. Wouldn't have recognized her if I hadn't read the map. 'Peace and harmony' was her message and that's what I've found, but I took the long road around. Didn't I tell you my future was predicted in the stars?"

"Yes, ma'am. You did," I agreed. "Where do you suppose old Pluto is off to now? Chasing cats?"

"Don't know. Don't care. He's not giving me trouble," she said. "Want some tea?"

I started toward the kitchen when she waved me away saying she'd make a pot herself, and that woman got up and walked as steady as you please to the kitchen. I didn't know whether to laugh or cry. "What does Thelma say about you being up and out?" I called to her.

"I don't see much of Thelma," she said cheerfully. "She comes home to change her clothes and out she goes again. The poor child is working her fingers to the bone, I do believe. It's the war, you know, keeping the plant fired up night and day."

"Uh-huh," I said, pretending I believed old Thelma was worked to a frazzle. On my way over, I'd seen her at the bank, waiting for Emory to come off his shift.

A stack of unopened letters was on the table. I knew by the handwriting they were from Dempsey and I was having a hard time resisting the temptation to grab them and run off. In fact, you know those letters *are* mine. I'm the one he's writing to even though he doesn't know it. I was relieved to read the Texas postmark because it means Dempsey is still on American soil. I haven't had a letter myself for weeks. That boy is breaking my heart.

Well, Mrs. Thompson brought us a pot of tea and went back for cups while I cleared the table to make room. "Isn't this nice!" she said. "I got you to thank, Bobby Lee. You visited me when I was my lowest. You introduced me to Tippy. I thank you, honey, for my life."

"You don't want to thank me," I said, funning her a little. "You want to thank your lucky stars."

"Oh, yes," she said, dead serious. "Oh, *yes*. I thank the stars above all."

"That's where they are," I said. She seemed to wait for

me to explain. "Above," I said, pointing upwards. "The stars *are* above all."

After that, I let it be. "You planning on marrying Mr. K.?" I said, getting down to brass tacks. I expected her to be embarrassed, but she looked me in the eye.

"When he teaches me mind reading," she said, like a sensible person, "I'll consider an offer of marriage."

"Well," I said, "how long will that be?"

"Soon, I suspect," she said confidently.

"Congratulations," I said. I didn't know whether or not to mention the subject of bigamy. His *and* hers. Suppose Mr. Thompson showed up. What then? "I wish you all the luck in the world, Mrs. Thompson, I really do."

"Oh, honey, I don't need luck. The stars have it planned. Tippy and I are moving in the same orbit. We'll be just fine."

I had all the conversation about stars I could take for one day. "I have to be getting back," I said and put my empty cup back in its saucer.

"Come again," she said and went to the door with me. "You writing them stories still?"

"Yes, ma'am," I said.

"Glad to hear it."

Mrs. Thompson made a pretty sight in the doorway. She reminded me of Barbara Stanwyck again — Barbara Stanwyck waiting for Fred MacMurray to come knocking on the door, not to commit bigamy and murder, but to go off hand in hand into the sunset.

Time to write my usual Thelma letter to Dempsey. I'll write how I miss him and sleep with his letters under my pillow. Old Thelma doesn't, but I really do.

Do you think being a liar is worse than being a bigamist? Isn't it the same thing when you boil it down because someone always gets hurt?

Your ever-loving-lying friend,
B.L.

P.S. Rabbi Daniel gave me *Introduction to Judaism* to read. He said he'd talk to my parents if I wanted him to. I told him it wouldn't do any good—they were both deaf mutes. I could see by his face I hadn't helped my cause.

Twin Branch, Ky.
November 2, 1944

Dear Sue,

Here's one for the books—Thelma wants me to write Dempsey a "Dear John" letter. You know what a "Dear John" letter is, don't you? That's when you give a GI the heave-ho! That's awful, you know, but girls are doing it to GIs all over the country. They write "Dear John" and say they've found some other guy to love. It's an epidemic, but, look, Thelma will pay $2.

"Let Dempsey down easy," she said, shining her green lights. "'I still care for you. Sorta.'"

Tell the truth (how I wish you would!). Are you disappointed in me for doing this? It wouldn't be *only* for the money—if I don't write the letter, Thelma said *she* would and that would be a holy mess of hurt feelings.

Do you read the weekly *Grit*? The newspaper said girls who write "Dear John" letters are often terribly rude and insensitive and some GIs get so depressed they have to see a psychiatrist to help them through their misery. Two rules to follow, the story said, are: (1) use a *positive tone;* (2) do *not* be *personally critical.*

Thelma says, "Tell him I need someone on the premises to care for. I'm not a long-distance sort of person." I might write those exact words. That is the truth.

I wish I knew for certain Dempsey loves Thelma. I don't know what he sees in her besides the fact she's good-looking. She didn't finish high school. Of course, nobody has to have an education to get a job when there's a war going on. Nobody has to be Einstein to work at the Triple H. It's a fact a person working in a defense plant makes more money than a college professor.

I've been thinking about working at the Triple H when I graduate. I told Miss Watkins, who looked so mad, I expected her to smack me in the face. I was about to say, "You think you're my mother? Well, Rose has never laid a hand on me and you better not, either."

Miss Watkins makes no bones about my going to college. She's taken to pushing me on my science and math, and I know she wants me to read her daddy's entire library. She wants me to take the acceleration classes. If I did, I could graduate a year ahead of my class. I'd be the only girl to graduate. Acceleration is aimed at boys busting their breeches to go to war.

"I'm in no big hurry," I told Miss Watkins because, sure, I'm planning to leave Twin Branch someday, but I'm not sure exactly when. Spring might be too soon. Who said I wanted to *go* to college?

"I went to college when I was 16," she said.

"I'm not like you," I said, wishing I had the nerve to add, "throwing my life away for a Comma."

I'm trying not to think about Miss Watkins and how she carries on the way she does about college. My daddy isn't going to send me to college. That's that.

Do you remember the essay I wrote for Thelma for the movie-star contest and never sent because Emory never paid for her picture? Maybe I'll put some of it in Dempsey's "Dear John" letter. I'll plagiarize myself. Remember I said Thelma's "thing to love" is Hollywood? That's what I'll tell Dempsey. "Sorry, Dempsey, old thing, but I don't love you anymore, I'm loving Hollywood and packing my bags tonight…" Awfully rude, right?

Strange doings—Thelma paying me to pay you. Like I always say, "No one can predict the future." I think the situation is called "ironic."

Ain't it the truth?

Your everlasting friend,
B.L.

Twin Branch, Ky.
November 10, 1944

Dear Sue,

I can't believe Clay Fanin paid Thelma an unknown amount of money to break off with Dempsey, but he did.

Thelma told me so herself. Bragging, mind you!

"That means I lied to Dempsey," I said, because I wrote Dempsey what she said about needing a boyfriend on the premises and everyone knows Emory is who she has in mind.

"No, you didn't lie. It was *after* I mailed the letter I got the call. I do need a guy who's here and not flying an airplane a thousand miles away. Emory said I should have told Dempsey to go chase himself a long time ago. Look," she said, hands on her hips, "getting a check from Dempsey's daddy wasn't my idea. He talked like I had a rope around Dempsey's neck, leading him on. 'Here's the money to let go,' he told me.

"Well, O.K., beats working."

"He bribed you for nothing," I said, but not really minding someone getting the better of old Clay.

"Do you think he'd send more money if I asked him?"

"Then *you'd* be blackmailing *him*!" I hollered at her. "Don't you have any scruples?"

"So?" she said. "Big deal."

"If you do, I'll write Dempsey everything," I warned her, but thinking I should mind my own business. Then I said to myself, *Dempsey is my business.*

"Including the part about *you* writing *my* letters?" Thelma said in a nasty way. You know how ugly she can be. "See how he feels about you lying!"

That did it! I said, "Including the part about you and Emory being lovebirds."

She stopped in her tracks and put a big old grin on

her face. "You wouldn't tell, would you?" Sweet-talking me, you know.

"What do you think?" I said, but I wasn't sure I would.

"Miss Snoop, you should forget all about writing and go into the detective business. You're pretty good," Thelma said, as cheerfully as could be. "You visited my mama lately?"

"Maybe next week."

"Mama sure likes you," she said. "I'm getting jealous."

"Of me? You'd be the only person in the world," I assured her.

We had this easy conversation at Rexall's with Thelma drinking black coffee and me a Dr. Pepper. Her face looked a little peaked. She had gained some extra pounds, tightening the skirt, already a mite too tight. Don't get me wrong—she hadn't lost her looks. If she had, I'd be trying to find them.

We finally ran out of talk. Thelma gave me a flip Bette Davis "See you around," followed by a no-hard-feelings smile. If we'd been men, we might have shook hands and gone our separate ways. We parted on pretty good terms. I saw Thelma and me, maybe, being friends in a way we'd never been—real girlfriends who shared secrets, not just because we had no one else to tell them to.

Well, I have you. I can tell you secrets if I want and do. You don't tell my secrets, do you? You wouldn't, would you? You haven't, have you? How will I know?

Waiting ever patiently,
B.L.

Dear Sue,

I'm working on Lesson #5: *Characterization*. It says: "Illuminate an aspect of a chosen character engaged in a racking conflict of their daily existence." I figure it means someone like Sylvia. I bumped into her today at the WPA Library. I'd come for John Steinbeck. Last week I saw *The Grapes of Wrath* at the "X" and now I can't wait to read the book. Well, from the pained look on Sylvia's face I knew I'd chosen the right character. She was bent over the *Cincinnati Post*.

"The *Twin Branch Independent* isn't good enough for *you*, huh?" I said, joking because no one reads the local paper except for church news and weddings. I should have known better than joke with Sylvia when she's in a *racking* mood.

"A person has to keep up with the news," she said without looking at me. "It's a duty every American citizen has in wartime."

"You're right," I said to butter her up a bit for my assignment. "Absolutely."

"People in town don't take their duties seriously. They're making money from the war. They don't want to read about suffering. They don't want to know the casualties."

"Be fair, Sylvia," I said, loud enough so Miss Fish, the librarian, put a finger to her lips. "You're not the only person on the green earth to read city newspapers. I do when I'm not reading books or writing about racking experiences of interesting characters. My daddy does. A lot of people in this town do." I was making this into a federal case, but the truth is Sylvia is right — hands down.

"Tell me all about it, Bobby Lee." Sylvia was real sarcastic now. "After this *informed* population do their reading, you know what else they do? They write insulting letters to the only Jewish family in town. Tell me about the informed people who hate Jews."

Every time Sylvia gets excited like that, I get sick to my stomach. *I* end up feeling like the war is *my* fault. To make matters worse, today Sylvia accused Fritzie and Sophie (said it right out loud) of being German spies! Because they are my friends, I feel guilty about that, too!

"They talk in German so no one will know their secrets," she told me.

"They are from Germany, Sylvia. What would you expect? Chinese? Everybody in America comes from someplace else or their ancestors did. Except for Indians, and some people say the Indians did, too."

Sylvia wasn't listening to me. She's so stubborn! What else is new, huh? "I bet they have pictures of Hitler on their walls," she said. "I bet they salute and say 'Heil Hitler' a hundred times a day."

I've been to the Becker house and can swear there are no pictures of Hitler on the walls. I told her. "They are really nice," I said. "Mr. Becker was Boy Scout leader for 2 years until he was asked to resign."

"Because he's a German spy," Sylvia said, nodding.

"He's *not* a spy," I said. "But, well, it might have been

because he is German." Sylvia isn't the only person in town to suspect the Beckers.

I hate arguing with Sylvia. She's so *obsessed*.

Later today she was leaning against the lamp pole across from Fredrick's Bootery.

"What are you doing here?"

"Watching," she said.

"You spotted any enemy planes dropping secret plans to Fritzie?" I asked her. "You know you've lost your marbles, don't you?"

"If you were sincere about being a Jew, you'd take the matter seriously."

"I do," I said, "but what has that to do with you standing here like a jerk? What does your daddy say?"

"He's afraid to start anything," she said.

"What's to start?" I said, starting the argument again. "Come on, Sylvia, can you honestly see nice Mr. Becker hurting anybody?"

"Grow up, Bobby Lee!" Sylvia growled. "Life isn't like the movies. You can't tell the bad guys from the good guys by looking at them." Then she pulled a wrinkled envelope from her pocket and handed it to me.

I unfolded the paper inside. It was handwritten. The letter writer called the Weinstocks liars and thieves, and members of a conspiracy to rule the world. I counted "Jew-bastard" 10 times, and, well, other stuff I can't put down on paper. When I finished, my stomach was like a tight fist. Sylvia must feel angry like this all the time.

"The guy is a nut. Crazy" was all I could think to say. I gave the letter back, glad to be rid of it. I wondered how

147

a guy who could spell and use punctuation, you know, as if he were *educated*, could believe the garbage he wrote. "He's crazy," I said.

"You should read the other letters."

"There are more?"

"Every day another comes in the mail," Sylvia said, peering at a postmark we both knew was Twin Branch.

"Sylvia, I swear you're wrong about Fritzie and Sophie. They couldn't write those letters," I said. "They can't write. They don't know how to write English. I write their letters," I said. "Don't spread it around. They'd be embarrassed."

Did I tell you how I write all kinds of letters for the Beckers? I cancel orders and complain about poor merchandise. It is sort of fun. Most of their business is by telephone. For something special, though, the Beckers dictate to me—their personal secretary.

Without a word, Sylvia put the letter in her pocket and we started toward the Bon Ton, both of us staring suspiciously at every person we passed. I couldn't help it and I knew she couldn't either. Did that one write the letters or that one? When people do ordinary things, like running errands and shopping, you can't see the hate they carry with them. They act as ordinary as the rest of us. Before the war, Germans probably acted ordinary, going about their business, too, but now Nazis torture people and kill them and act like fiends from another planet!

"Who'd have thought humans could be so evil, so full of hate?" I said.

"My father says only small-minded people hate."

"I never actually *hated* hillbillies, you know," I said,

fearing she'd think I was a small-minded person for the way I sometimes blow off about hillbillies.

"I never took you seriously," she said.

"I'm beginning to think no one takes me seriously."

"You don't have the heart for it."

"I'm not small-minded, right?" I wanted to hear her say it.

"I bet everybody in town knows who writes those letters, but no one will say," Sylvia said. "*Including* you, Bobby Lee."

With that, she disappeared in the Bon Ton and I started to boil inside. She can have her suspicions of people around here, but why lump me with them? What did I do? What have those letters to do with me, a person who loves gefilte fish?

You know, the sooner I get out of this town, the better.

Seriously,
B.L.

Twin Branch, Ky.
November 21, 1944

Dear Sue,

Guess where Dempsey is? The Pacific! Wouldn't you know? He wants to fight Nazis and he gets the Japs, people who kill themselves if they have a bad day. Dempsey says he's disappointed having to fight about islands. He was on one when he wrote the letter, waiting for orders. I hope it wasn't Leyte. Leyte is where the worst fighting goes on. I know Dempsey wishes he were with Eisenhower, not General MacArthur, but nobody asked him to pick his general.

I can hardly bring myself to tell you what he said about the "Dear John" letter. He's *forgiven* her! He said, "She's a wise and sensible person, and a really good writer, too. It must be why I fell for her in the first place."

Oh, brother! My dandruff flew up! I even told Miss Watkins about this tacky situation I got myself into, and, you know, I swore I'd never tell her another secret. She did what you'd expect. She went straight to her bookcase. "Read this." She gave me a play to read this time: *Cyrano de Bergerac.* Like I told you, I can't say no to Miss Watkins, so I read about a guy with a nose like Jimmy Durante's and about as good-looking as he is, who agreed to write love letters for his friend to the girl they both loved. It's true — this guy and I were in the same predicament because the girl liked the handsome friend who couldn't write worth a dime. Well, I read about Cyrano like he was my long-lost twin. I hope I have better luck winning Dempsey's heart, especially since Thelma is always with Emory. They are always together — *close* together — except when they do their separate shifts at the Triple H.

Poor Dempsey is getting the short end of the stick when it comes to loving Thelma. When he comes home from the war, he might be changed. He's changed some already. "The war isn't how I thought it would be," he wrote in a letter to me. It said, "I hate flying!"

Why do boys have to fight wars old men start? Mrs. Brammer is not the only one with a Gold Star hanging in her window any longer. Stars shine from other windows in town. Mr. Gallings lost his favorite nephew in the Pacific and wouldn't talk to a soul for a week. Not even to me!

I think I wrote that the high school is holding a special graduation in March so the senior boys can have their diplomas before they are dragged off to the armed forces. Miss Watkins is pressuring me to graduate with those guys. I have the extra credits. I could start college this summer, she says.

I asked her, "What makes you think my daddy would let me go?" She didn't bother answering me. I feel pity for Daddy when Miss Watkins gets hold of him. Once she makes up her mind even my daddy will have a hard time arguing.

Funny thing is, Daddy doesn't need me, not since Charley's been coming here on weekends. Daddy calls him "Sonny" like in "Son," you know? Daddy must have been real disappointed when he first laid eyes on me at Johns Hopkins. Rose was probably too busy reading about Hedy Lamarr to notice the tears spilling over and trickling down his cheeks. Girls don't get an even amount of respect with boys, not even when they're the ones having the babies and doing the chores. I hate that, don't you?

I can't believe I actually kissed Charley. What came over me? *You* know. You know everything and say nothing. Tell me how Dempsey can dream about Thelma while I'm pining away for him. *That's* what came over me.

Your down-in-the-dumps friend,
B.L.

Twin Branch, Ky.
November 22, 1944

Dear Sue,

Wave Good-bye! Mrs. Thompson and Mr. K. left Twin Branch in a 1940 Buick from Troy's used-car lot. The initials C.F. were engraved in gold letters on the door. I asked Troy if they stood for Clay Fanin, but Troy wouldn't tell.

Bill Farley married them. I didn't know a sheriff could do that, did you? No one present objected, and I knew better than to speak up. The ceremony was quick as a door slam. Daddy and I were the witnesses. Farley read the Lord's Prayer and Mrs. Thompson and Mr. K. said "I do" to the question that began "Will you take…" and that was that.

Thelma didn't come. Her lame excuse was having to work that shift. How about that? All those months, complaining about her mama in bed, and she doesn't show for the celebration! You'd think that girl would be dancing in the street.

"I can't understand you, Thelma," I said. "Sigmund Freud couldn't understand you."

"Go fly a kite," she told me, showing off her usual wit.

If you ask me, Thelma's bluff has been called and she's sorry Mrs. Thompson is out of bed and being normal. She had *resigned* herself to Mrs. Thompson's ways. It was how she got attention (and money!) from the guys at the bank, too, because, like everyone else, they felt sorry for Thelma's predicament. (How do you like that? I may be better than Freud!)

The fact is Thelma didn't miss much of a wedding. We drank ginger ale in the sheriff's office. He had Ritz crackers and Velveeta cheese, and I did the spreading. The wedding appeared to be a spur-of-the-moment thing. If I'd known they were going to pull this stunt, I'd have made Daddy put out money for a wedding cake with trimmings, the way a wedding is supposed to be. Besides me, Mr. K. has no friends in town, unless you call my daddy his friend. Good thing for Mr. K. Charley came to town. Otherwise, my daddy could have been in a nasty mood about severance pay. No matter—the wedding couple announced their plan to drive to St. Louis, Mo., right after the ceremony. Mr. K. had a telegram delivered to him that morning. He only flashed it at us, but I could read it was from the Missouri State Theater.

"You learned mind reading, didn't you?" I said to *Mrs.* K.

"Honey, it was easy as pie," she said.

"Now you're going on the stage of that state theater. You scared?"

"Not at all. Not one bit. I've learned Automatic Mind Command, too."

Mrs. K. explained to me she can now control a person's thoughts and actions without them knowing it. She can tell them what to say and what to do. It's Automatic Mind Command. She discovered AMC in one of her astrology magazines.

"You aren't controlling *my* mind now, are you?" I asked, because I suddenly felt lightheaded.

"Well, it's kind of a secret. I'm not supposed to talk about it with the *uninitiated*."

That was O.K. with me. Mrs. K. said she cut out a coupon from one of the astrology magazines Thelma brings her, then sent it to Buffalo, New York, with a $5 bill Mr. K. donated. AMC arrived within the week with instructions and three small white marbles. That was all she was allowed to tell me. "The AMC folks have strict rules," she said.

I was glad.

Mrs. K. was married in a white satin dress, bought that morning from the Bon Ton. She wore those snappy shoes Mr. K. bought from Fritzie. Mr. K. wore the plaid suit he had ordered special from New York the first day he started work at the SG. He must have thought the SG was a classier store than it turned out to be. The suit was never worn. He said it was waiting for him to fall in love again. (Oh, brother!)

Before Mr. and Mrs. K. took off, I tied artificial flowers and blue and pink ribbons on the back of the car. Then they were on the road headed west, sort of married, you could say.

I miss them already. I missed them beginning the very second the car turned the corner, leaving me behind.

Thanks to my daddy, Charley Burt is here to stay as Mr. K.'s substitute. Charley quit the school in Boone Hollow and will be moving into Mr. K.'s old boarding house. In case you're curious, Charley isn't thinking about that kiss on the hill any more than I am. His mind is strictly on business. I'm not complaining because, look, my daddy's happy, and Rose is happy, too. She says Charley reminds her of a tall Mickey Rooney. He sort of does. I never liked

Mickey Rooney. I like Judy Garland, of course, but not when she's matched with Mickey Rooney.

This town feels empty without the Wedding Couple. Don't get me wrong, I'm glad Mrs. Thompson, now Mrs. K., is out of bed and Mr. K. has a partner. I'm not feeling sorry for myself either. I feel deserted is all—like when Dempsey left.

The SG's closing for the day. Charley's spreading muslin over the pants. It's time to stop thinking about Mr. and Mrs. K. and say, "Good-bye, old friends," to the happy couple and, "Hope you don't run into Shirley."

Imagine the two of them, free as birds, flying a thousand miles away. After St. Louis, who knows? Mrs. K. might make it to China yet. No one can predict the future.

Your wedding reporter,
Bobby Lee

Twin Branch, Ky.
November 30, 1944

Dear Sue,

The G.A.W.S. package arrived today! According to my figures I still owe your daddy (?) $2.50. So why the rest of the Writing Lessons? What goes? Is this your doings again? I've got to believe it is. I think it is the *sign* I've been waiting for all these months. My premonitions about you were right. You do care about me. You *are* my friend. You just happen to be a rotten pen pal!

If that is true—why was my last letter returned? Stamped on the envelope was *Return to Sender*. On this letter, Mr. Gallings said to write: *Please Forward (if necessary)* in red ink, which I'm going to do. He says a letter would follow you to California and back if I write *Please Forward* on it.

You aren't in California, are you? Miss Watkins holds the theory that you are a figment of my imagination. Today, when I returned her book of short stories by Saki (another nom de plume!), she said there is no G.A.W.S.

"Your Writers School is a box number," she has pointed out more than a hundred times. "It is not an address on a street anybody's heard of."

Miss Watkins likens G.A.W.S. to the story of *The Wizard of Oz*. You know, by L. Frank Baum? It was made into a movie starring Judy Garland, and Frank Morgan played the Wizard. I loved it.

"It is more than possible that your Writers School is a one-man operation," she said, "with Buckley himself stuffing and stamping the envelopes."

You, she figured, are the bookkeeper. "If Sue exists at all," she said.

She's wrong. I've always known in my heart you're a real person and a good friend. It's a feeling deep inside of me, and receiving the lessons you've sent proves me right. Miss Watkins is not one to back down on her opinions, but she'll have to as soon as she sees what you sent. I wish you had added a note with something personal—anything. How about: "Dear B.L., Good luck with Dempsey. I'm still searching for my thing to love." Well, you know what I mean—something *revealing* I can show Miss Watkins.

I am thinking of calling it quits with her. I must have read 200 of the books she's selected. After I read one, she wants to know what I think. If I say, "I liked it," she'll say, "Why?" If I say, "I didn't like it," she'll say, "Why?" One way or another I have to tell her why. I hate that.

Right now I'm reading *Pudd'nhead Wilson* by Mark Twain. (Isn't Mark Twain the best nom de plume in the world?) The story is *ironic*. (I'm getting used to the word.) It's about an *arrogant* man who thinks he's white and doesn't know he's legally a slave, and a man who everyone thinks is a slave who *is* white and is heir to riches. The so-called dope, Pudd'nhead Wilson, solves a murder mystery that sets the facts straight and shows how foolish people can be in their thinking about the white and black races. Well, that's the gist of it. It's a good book. (Don't ask why!)

As soon as I finished reading *Pudd'nhead*, I found Annie Sturges in the kitchen and handed it to her. "This is right up your alley," I told her. "Remember what I said about you coming to Baltimore with me? Nobody would know you were colored. You could go anywhere in the city you pleased—eat in any restaurant you wanted. Ride up front with the streetcar conductor without a soul knowing," I said, making my case.

"No, thank you, honey," Annie said. "I know you mean well, but I'm not ashamed of being a Negro. My mama never taught me shame, no ma'am. Now, give me your hand."

I did.

"I do declare," she said, studying my palm as usual. "I think you're going to amount to something."

When Annie told me she wasn't interested in *Pudd'nhead*, I left it on the kitchen table. Later, it was gone, as I suspected it would be. Annie had it in the basement where the porch glider stays in the winter. She reads there, in private, when she wants. During the day there's no one to take notice of it except me.

Did you hear Lowell Thomas say the GIs will be out of the Pacific soon? It was a report from the War Department, but I'm not getting my hopes up. The Japanese aren't surrendering by the thousands the way the Nazis are in Europe.

Daddy said, "Where are we going to put all those Nazi prisoners?"

"Put them in concentration camps with Jews as guards," I said. I'm sounding a lot like Sylvia, who, by the way, told me her cousin Lore came to her in a dream and told her to become a rabbi. She says she will. The Jesus Serves church has two women preachers. They can dip people in the river, baptizing them in the Big Sandy, as well as the men. Of course, a female rabbi is something else again.

"Can you?" I asked her, meaning "Is it allowed?"

"I don't know," she said. "Rabbi Daniel said he had never heard of it happening. H.U.C. has no females studying."

"Maybe you can't," I said.

"I'll protest," she said.

She will, too. I'll let you know how it turns out.

Meanwhile, I've got a secret to tell you, but I won't until I see whether or not this letter has *Return* printed on the envelope. I'm not wasting a good, juicy secret going nowhere. Aren't you curious? Write as soon as you get this letter or you'll be sorree!

Here, waiting on you!
B.L.

Twin Branch, Ky.
December 2, 1944

Dear Sue,

You win! I couldn't wait. I *had* to write. Thelma is pregnant! She's telling folks it's Dempsey's baby, but everyone in town knows it's Emory's. Thelma wants Mr. Fanin to pay the doctor bills. She's already telling the town that her baby is the heir to the Fanin fortune. Sylvia says, "That girl's got *chutzpah*." After she explained what it meant I agreed. (Did I tell you Sylvia is trying to teach me some Yiddish? She is. I asked for it.)

My personal opinion is Thelma took the idea from *Ma Perkins*, the soap opera. The plot has been going on for months: soldier boy's daddy is being blackmailed by son's lying old flame.

It is pretty corny, even for the plot of a Thelma story. She's been living with Emory in the house on Pollard Road, like a normal human (except for not being married), so why is she starting something now, I'd like to know.

"We're happy as clams," she told me herself. "Emory's mama kicked him out, and that's fine with us because he doesn't have to give her a penny."

It's shameful for her to ask Dempsey's daddy to fork over money she doesn't even need. Now I'm feeling sorry for Mr. Fanin. He wouldn't know if Dempsey is to blame. Of course, I would. I've kept track, don't you know. Thelma isn't mean. She's greedy. If her daddy hadn't run off, she might have been as honorable as you or me. (You are, aren't you?)

I'm writing all of this because I knew you'd be interested. I should be sending it to *True Confessions*. I might still. Thelma says things like, "God help me! What do I need a baby for?" and then she'll pat her stomach. "What's going on in there?" she'll say, real cute. "You having a party?"

Thelma says she doesn't care if I tell Dempsey the truth about those letters I've been writing for her. I'm not telling. Not yet. I'll wait until he comes home. Thelma might change her mind. People change. For example, take my daddy. Yesterday he said to me, "You don't have to hang around here. I don't need you *and* Sonny."

"How's that again? Did I hear you correctly?" I said.

"Go on. Take your time," Daddy said, nice as you please. "I know you want a Coke with your friends. Go on."

This morning I asked Annie Sturges to take another look at my hand. "Something weird is happening in my life. What is it?"

"Well, well," said Annie, stringing me along, giving herself time to think it over. "I do see something—a funny line around your thumb. Never saw that before."

"So?"

"Smoky. Like train smoke," she said. "Looks like you going on a trip. *Baltimore,* I do believe."

"Mind reader extraordinaire" I said, applauding. She knows Baltimore is my plan. "You sure like having fun with me."

"I do," she agreed. "We still friends?"

"You might be my one and only."

Annie never tells me what I want to hear. I don't expect she can. Butterflies circle inside me announcing something special is going to happen, but what? *You* write *me*? I used to pretend that you looked forward to my letters and smiled when the mailman dropped one on your desk. Now I'm wondering if you haven't been dropping them in the garbage as fast as they arrived.

I hope not.

No matter—the vital sign was your sending the Lessons. I'll always remember that. I've *analyzed* them. On my English term paper I wrote, "Guy de Maupassant is strong on plot that, from the beginning of his stories, carries the reader impulsively along." (Lesson #6: *The Plot as Action!*) Miss Watkins flipped like a nickel when she read that.

Now—this is serious—I've been writing to you, off and on, for almost a year. The question in my mind is: Has the time come to say *good-bye*? Do you want me to? I tell myself if Sue were interested in me as a person, she would have written by this time. Besides sending the Lessons, wasn't there something else to add?

So—O.K.! I'm sorry—this is, definitely, my last letter. I assume you want it this way.

Your friend now and forever,
Bobby Lee

Twin Branch, Ky.
December 26, 1944

The Great American Writers School
P.O. Box 140
Kokomo, Indiana

Dear Sirs:

Does Susan Buckley still work for you? Your President, Mr. Henry W. Buckley, is either her daddy or her husband. I never knew which. I've been writing to her at this address for almost a year, but lately the letters are rubber-stamped "Return to Sender."

If you have any information as to her whereabouts, anything at all, I'd appreciate your writing to me here in Twin Branch. That's all you have to write on the envelope. Mr. Gallings, the postmaster, knows where to find me.

Sincerely yours,
Bobby Lee Pomeroy

Twin Branch, Ky.
January 30, 1945

The Great American Writers School
P.O. Box 140
Kokomo, Indiana

Dear Sirs:

I wrote to you some weeks ago about Miss (or Mrs.) Susan Buckley. I always wrote to her at this address and then some

162

letters came back with "Return to Sender" printed on the envelope. I sent them off again and don't know what happened to them.

If you come across Sue, would you deliver a message? Tell her I'm taking the acceleration program at the high school and will graduate in March with the guys going in the armed forces. Tell her *I'm* not going into the armed forces, but my teacher, Miss Watkins, says I have the credits to enter college, and that's what I'm going to do. Also, tell her Sylvia Weinstock changed her mind about being a rabbi. She plans to join the WACs. Sue will want to know about that.

As for Sue and me—well—I might have made her feel bad about not answering my letters. I wanted to know her. I am a curious person. I was born that way. Tell her I apologize and not to think I'm bitter, because I'm not. Sue and Henry were good friends to me while they lasted.

Sincerely yours,
Bobby Lee Pomeroy

Bobby Lee Pomeroy
Twin Branch, Kentucky
April 7, 1945

Dear Miss Pomeroy:

Congratulations! You are about to be published!

A copy of the book, *Letters from My Kentucky Home*, could be coming your way, straight off our press!

You could be the proud owner of a collection of *your own writing*, handsomely bound, privately printed on the modern presses of the *Vainglory Publishing Company*.

Only ten dollars ($10) is needed to cover the cost of printing and binding. Additional copies can be had for as little as five dollars ($5) each. The amount *must be paid in advance*. We are certain you, *the authoress*, will want many copies of this book to sell or to give as gifts to your family, friends, and neighbors.

Write your check or money order for ten dollars ($10) or MORE. Payable to *Vainglory Publishing Company* at the address below.

Mail it *promptly!*

Thanking you in advance, we hope you will keep the *Vainglory Publishing Company* in mind for future publishing ventures.

You obviously have the new, fresh, lively talent that every publisher seeks. This small amount ($10) is a BIG INVESTMENT in your future.

Yours truly,
GEORGE BAILEY, PRESIDENT
VAINGLORY PUBLISHING COMPANY
P.O. BOX 141, KOKOMO, INDIANA

April 21, 1945

Dear Mr. Bailey:

My mother forwarded your letter to me at school from my home in Twin Branch, Ky. When I read it, I thought I was having a bad case of what the French call *déjà vu*. Your proposition is mighty tempting, but I can't spare $10 and I suspect you don't have an installment plan.

Thanks again for the offer — strange as I find it!

Sincerely yours,

Miss Bobbi Lee Pomeroy
Women's Dormitory
University of Cincinnati
Cincinnati, Ohio

Epilogue

At spring break, in my sophmore year at the University of Cincinnati, I rode a Greyhound bus to Kokomo, Indiana. With the help of Mr. Gallings at the post office, I was able to trace the address of the owner of Boxes 140 and 141 and finally arrived at a two-story red brick house. Above the bell was a neatly printed card: *The Great American Writers School*. Underneath, in the same print on another card: *Vainglory Publishing Company*.

I pressed the bell and was met by a woman with wavy blond hair down to her shoulders and the creamiest complexion I'd ever seen this side of a Jergens Lotion ad. She wasn't young, but she wasn't old either. I said the first thing that came to mind, "Ginger Rogers!" and she burst out laughing.

"Who are you looking for?" she asked.

"Henry or Sue Buckley," I said. Her smile began to fade. "Do you know where I could find them? I'm a friend. Honest."

"Who are you, kid?" she demanded.

"Bobbi Lee Pomeroy from Twin Branch, Kentucky," I said.

She burst out laughing again, opened the screen door and, fastening onto my arm, pulled me inside. "I'm Winona Miklovich. Glad to meet you."

Winona scrambled us eggs for lunch that we ate on a table in the messy but comfortable living room where stacks of Writing Lessons were piled in the corners, *Writers Guides* along the walls, and G.A.W.S. stationery— "Dear _____" (to be typed in)—cluttered a desk.

Winona, alias Susan Buckley, told me how she and her

husband, Jack, used Buckley as their nom de plume. They were high school teachers before they established G.A.W.S. for fun and profit, but when Jack was killed at Pearl Harbor, Winona decided to carry on alone.

"I write Henry Buckley letters the way he would have," she told me. "It keeps him alive for me. I sign letters *Susan Buckley* to remind me that *I'm* alive."

"That's so sad," I said sincerely.

"Oh, look, honey, life goes on, you know," she said and patted my hand.

We talked the afternoon away like old friends. She had questions about Thelma, so I told her Thelma had a baby girl, named Adeline.

"Thelma married Emory and calmed herself down," I said.

"And Sylvia?" she asked.

Sylvia was in college in New York with a new plan to study law. "Things changed for the Weinstocks when the hate mail and calls stopped," I said. "There hasn't been any since November 22, 1944, the day Mr. K. left town," I said, though it pained me.

"And, now, Dempsey?" she said, expecting something different, I suspected, than what I told her.

Dempsey had come home safe from the war and attends the University of Kentucky as his daddy wanted. He plans to be a veterinarian. When he returned, out of uniform, I knew he could never be my Romeo nor I his Juliet. I was in college, with other fish to fry. I heard he's engaged to a girl who teaches school in Paris (Paris, *Kentucky*, that is).

Then I asked her what had been heavy on my mind.

"Why didn't you answer my letters?"

"You still thinking about that? Oh, honey, I was too busy, living hand to mouth, to answer letters. Your Miss Watkins had me pegged," she said. "I am a wizard, not of Oz, but with these." She pointed to a Woodstock typewriter and an old mimeograph machine.

Seeing my disappointment, she patted my hand. "You didn't need me. You knew your grammar and punctuation. Thanks to your Miss Watkins, you read good books by good writers. I sent you all the Lessons. What was left for me to say? You know no one could predict the future."

"You could have been a friend," I said, a little bitter.

"I was. Only I was quiet about it."

Before I left, Winona gave me a package. "It's been waiting for you," she said and hugged me warmly. I hugged back, forgiving her, already putting her in the past — another character for another story.

When the bus crossed the Indiana state line, I opened her present. It wasn't "handsomely bound," and I doubt that it was printed by a "modern press," but I was thrilled. I had been published.

Letters from My Kentucky Home *by Bobby Lee Pomeroy, copyright © 1945 by Bobby Lee Pomeroy, All rights reserved, including the right of reproduction in whole or in part in any form. Published by arrangement with* Vainglory Publishing Company.

...Which brought to me *Lesson #11*—the one I learned on my own: a writer writes where there is space. A writer writes what she knows best. Whether it is a story or a poem or even a letter, the person who writes it is a writer.

By the way, this Lesson is free.